The Christmas Gazebo

Two Christmas Romances of past and present

The Christmas Gift by Marilyn Turk
The Christmas Surprise by Lenora Worth

Blessings,
Marilyn Turk

Copyright © 2019 by Marilyn Turk, Lenora Worth
Published by Forget Me Not Romances, an imprint of Winged Publications

Editor: Cynthia Hickey
Book Design by Winged Publications

All rights reserved. No part of this publication may be reproduced, stored in a retrieval system, or transmitted in any form or by any means—electronic, mechanical, photocopying, recording, or otherwise—without the prior written permission of the publisher. The only exception is brief quotations in printed reviews. Piracy is illegal. Thank you for respecting the hard work of this author.

This book is a work of fiction. Names, characters, Places, incidents, and dialogues are either products of the author's imagination or used fictitiously.
Any resemblance to actual persons, living or dead, or events is coincidental.

Christmas Holiday Romance
Christmas Romance
Contemporary Romance

ISBN-13: 978-1-947523-72-2

The Christmas Gift by Marilyn Turk — Page 1
The Christmas Surprise by Lenora Worth — Page 91

These stories are dedicated to DeFuniak Springs, Florida. While our stories are fiction and our characters are make-believe, the setting and some of the history of Springlake is loosely based on this beautiful Panhandle town that celebrates life with zeal and faith.

Defuniak Springs has a rich history and, yes, it still has a round lake and beautiful turn-of-the-century homes mixed in with quaint cottages and modern-day houses. And it still has the Chautauqua Assembly Building where people gather to enjoy and discuss art, education, recreation and spirituality.

We enjoyed talking to and learning from Carla Brown about the history of the best small town in Florida. Thank you, Carla, and Defuniak Springs. These stories are a love letter to you!

Marilyn Turk
Lenora Worth

The Christmas Gift
By Marilyn Turk

Chapter One

Springlake, Florida
November 1910

"Sir, there's someone on your property down by the lake." Samuel, the family butler, stood at the third-floor tower window gazing out.

Jonathon Townsend glanced up from the massive carved mahogany desk, welcoming the distraction from going over legal papers.

"Probably just some fishermen. Please send someone down there and ask them to stay off the property."

"Begging your pardon, sir, but I don't think that's a fisherman."

"Early guests for the Springlake Assembly already? Clearly, they can see where the path by the lake ends and our fence begins."

"Perhaps, sir."

Jonathon raised his eyebrows at the butler's tone, his curiosity piqued. He pushed away from the desk and joined Samuel by the window. The butler pointed. "There."

Jonathon picked up the binoculars sitting nearby and aimed them in the direction indicated. Sure enough, down by the water's edge stood a person, a woman. What was she doing? And what was that thing she wrestled with?

He lowered the binoculars. "Hmm. That's curious."

"Shall I have her sent away?"

"No, I need to stretch my legs. I'll go down there myself. I'd like to find out her intentions."

Jonathon donned his bowler and pulled on his jacket, trotted down to the second floor, took the grand staircase to the grand foyer, then through the solarium to the rear veranda. He squinted to peer through the trees behind the house. Where did she go? There, he spotted her at the water's edge.

He hurried down the steps to the hedges that surrounded the house before stepping into the formal garden and weaving his way through the maze of brick walkways. When he exited the garden, he saw her still fifty yards away. She bent over, then stood, then leaned over again, seemingly at odds with a piece of equipment in front of her.

As he drew closer, he realized the equipment was a camera on a tripod. She even appeared to be talking to it, frowning as if it were an uncooperative employee. He chuckled at the scene. When he was within earshot, he cleared his throat.

"Is it talking back?"

She spun around, eyes wide and mouth agape before understanding crossed her face.

"No, he's being quite contrary." She returned her attention to the camera.

Her straw boater with its black ribbon bow perched atop a bouffant of honey-colored hair. She was dressed in a practical manner wearing a fitted white blouse with puffed shoulders and slim arms paired with a sensible brown skirt displaying an incredibly small waist. Her matching jacket lay over a leather satchel sitting on the grass.

"I'm sorry. I didn't get your name." Jonathon moved around to the side of the camera trying to regain her attention.

She glanced up as if surprised he was still there. "I'm so

sorry. I didn't mean to be rude. Sometimes I get too engrossed in my work." She extended her hand. "I'm Loretta Morgan."

"Nice to meet you, Miss Morgan. My name is Jonathon Townsend."

Her forehead creased. "Townsend? Like the mercantile in town?"

He nodded. "The same."

Miss Morgan straightened. "And the lumber mill?"

He nodded again and smiled. "That too."

"Oh. My aunt mentioned you."

"And who is your aunt, if I may ask?"

"Aunt Gertie, I mean Mrs. Gertrude Ross. She lives over there." Miss Morgan pointed to a rooftop barely visible from their position beside the perfectly round lake.

"Yes, I know who Mrs. Ross is. She is very well-known around here. My parents have known her for years." He was quite familiar with the noted author who spent a few months a year at her cottage in Springlake. "Are you visiting her?"

"Yes, until I return home to the Catskills in New York or maybe go with her to her California home when she leaves here. Aunt Gertie loves the warm climate here, so my father allowed me to accompany her. He thought I needed a change of scenery."

Jonathon spread out his arms. "I'm sure this is quite different from the mountains."

"Certainly is." She glanced toward the lake as honking geese landed in the water with a swoosh and flapping of wings. "I'd love to capture the birds. In photographs, that is."

"And you're having problems with your camera? Perhaps I can help."

She faced him with her eyebrows lifted. "You know something about cameras?"

"A little. I believe we carry this model in our store. It's a Brownie, isn't it? It looks like the latest model Kodak has manufactured."

"It may not be the camera's fault, actually. I'm just having a hard time keeping it positioned on the tripod. Too bad the owner of this property doesn't have a dock or some place one could sit by the lake, something solid." She glanced toward his house sitting on the highest rise in the area, quite a distance from the lake. "I don't know why people would build their home on a lake and never come down to the water, just stay up there in their big fancy manor house and look out the windows."

Jonathon's ears warmed. "I suppose you're right."

She glanced at him, then covered her mouth with her hand. "Is that your house?"

He nodded and offered a weak smile. "It is."

"And this..." she swept her arms in a circle, "is your property?"

"It is." He bit back a laugh at her surprised look.

"I'm sorry. I didn't mean to trespass. I just wanted to get photographs from this perspective of the lake."

"That's quite all right. You're welcome to set your equipment here."

"Thank you. The waterfowl like to congregate in this area." A cacophony of quacks and honks nearby confirmed her statement. "I find them such fascinating subjects, God's creative display of art."

"You mentioned your work. Are you a professional photographer?"

Miss Morgan's face took on a rosy hue and she pursed her lips. "Not exactly. I mean, not yet."

"You're an apprentice, then?"

She twisted her mouth. "No. Not officially. I'm what you might call an independent-study."

"I see." But he didn't. The woman spoke in circles.

"Are you taking photographs for your aunt?"

Miss Morgan frowned. "Aunt Gertie?" She laughed. "I don't think Aunt Gertie is interested in photography. Now if

I were an artist who could sketch or paint the landscape, she'd be more interested. After all, those talents require skill."

The emphasis on the last word sent a tone of sarcasm mixed with disappointment.

"So I take it, you support the Photo Secession movement."

Her eyebrows lifted. "You're familiar with it? I'm not quite as avant garde as they are, but I do believe photography can produce artistic images."

He made an effort to lift her spirits. "I agree and believe taking good photographs requires skill too."

Her eyes widened and the prettiest smile lit her face. "You do? I'm so pleased to hear you say that. I've been trying to convince everyone else of that fact."

Jonathon's smile reflected hers as a warm sensation trickled through him. What a pleasant diversion from an otherwise boring afternoon. Unfortunately, the paperwork still waited his return. The whistle of an approaching train sounded from the depot on the opposite side of the lake, reminding him of the time. He retrieved his watch from his vest pocket to verify, aware that Mr. Farley from the bank would soon be arriving at the house for their appointment. He'd have to excuse himself, much as he preferred spending more time with the intriguing Miss Morgan.

"I'm sorry, but I must go. I have an appointment." An appointment that wouldn't be nearly as interesting as getting to know Miss Morgan.

"Of course. Please. I didn't mean to interrupt your schedule. You've been most kind." She offered her smile again as she straightened her skirt.

"Do you need help carrying your equipment back to your aunt's?"

"No, but thank you. Kody and I will be fine."

"Kody?" He glanced around. Had he overlooked someone?

She giggled and patted the camera. "Kody, my camera. We have a partnership, although sometimes he's an ornery partner."

Jonathon tipped his hat. "Then good day, Miss Morgan. And Kody." He turned and strode back to the house. Curious woman. But he certainly hoped she and 'Kody' would trespass on his property again.

So that's who owns the whole town. Lettie focused on the retreating form of Jonathon Townsend as he strode toward the grand Queen Anne mansion known as Magnolia Manor, its massive twin magnolias standing at attention like soldiers on either side. The house itself commanded the top of the hill like a Victorian castle, a wide veranda with gingerbread trim wrapping around three sides of the house with a glassed-in solarium facing the lake. On one side, a porte cochere allowed cars to pass through as they collected passengers or allowed them to disembark.

Jonathon Townsend was much younger than Loretta had envisioned when Aunt Gertie spoke of him. Not to mention handsome and well-built. And heir to the family businesses at such a young age! Just before she lost sight of him among the estate's garden, he turned and gave a slight wave.

Her face flushed, and she managed a little wave in return. He must've known she was watching him. She couldn't help it, though. The Townsend family name was all over the town of Springlake, and Aunt Gertie had referred to them with much respect. Lettie had pictured an austere, old, gray-haired man running all the businesses with an iron fist. Obviously, the man she'd just met was a descendant not much older than she.

What must he think of her, a stranger trespassing on his property? He'd been pleasant enough, but did he truly mean for her to return, or was he just being polite? She should discuss the matter with Aunt Gertie. With a start, Lettie realized it was time to go back to her aunt's house. She must be up from her nap by now.

Lettie put on her jacket, then collected her accessories, placing them in her satchel. She folded the tripod, stuck it under her arm, picked up the camera and satchel, and hiked up the hill in the direction of Tranquility, the cottage so named by her aunt as a reflection of the purpose of the cozy fall retreat. Unfortunately, Aunt Gertie's headaches persisted even at Tranquility, although less often, according to her aunt.

Lettie slipped inside the house, trying to be quiet and not disturb her aunt.

"Lettie? Is that you, dear?"

Lettie found Aunt Gertie in the parlor lying on the chaise. Setting down her equipment, she answered. "Yes, Aunt Gertie. I'm here. How are you feeling?"

"Better. Where have you been? Taking photographs, I assume?"

"Yes, ma'am, down by the lake. The ducks and geese are in abundance this time of year."

"Busy subjects, no doubt."

Lettie smiled. "They are indeed. It's difficult to get a photo that isn't blurred. I so wish I could take a photograph in color."

"Color? I never heard of that. Is it possible?"

Lettie shook her head. "Not that I know of." Lettie removed her jacket and tossed it over the back of the settee. "I met Mr. Jonathon Townsend down by the lake."

Aunt Gertie pushed up to a sitting position. "You did? By the water?"

"Yes. He's very nice."

"Yes, he is. Comes from a fine family. You know, his grandfather was one of the men that founded this town fifty years ago. He and two other men, all owners of the

Pensacola and Atlantic Railroad, were riding the train from Tallahassee to Pensacola, saw the lake and had the engineer stop the train. They got out and took a look at this beautiful place and decided it would be a perfect place for a town. So they built one! The man you met is Jonathon Townsend the Third. He took over management of the family businesses last year after his father passed away. I'm friends with his sweet mother, Annabelle."

"My goodness, they own a lot. He's rather handsome, don't you think?" A vision of the man's smile made her blush.

"Yes, he is. Most of the young women in town would love to get their hooks in him."

"I'm not surprised." Lettie pictured a swarm of women hovering over the man.

"But Annabelle thinks he'll settle down with Caroline, one of the Collier girls."

Lettie's heart sank, much to her dismay. But, why should that news matter to her? She didn't come to Springlake to find a husband. On the other hand, she hadn't expected to meet Jonathon Townsend either. No matter. All she wanted from him was the opportunity to use some of his lakefront property to take photographs. What the man did in his personal business did not concern her.

Chapter Two

"Caroline and her mother and sister will be arriving today," Mother said, as she worked on a needlepoint tapestry in the sunlit solarium.

"Hmm. That's nice." Jonathon sipped his coffee, then put his cup back on the table beside him as he studied the newspaper in his hand.

"I'm looking forward to hearing about their trip to London, aren't you?"

"That's nice." Jonathon continued reading an article.

"Jonathon! Are you listening to me?" The higher pitch in Mother's voice made him look up.

"Yes, Mother, what is it?"

She blew out a frustrated breath as she paused in her handwork. "Jonathon Townsend. Must you always have your head buried in some kind of paper? I said that Caroline Collier was arriving today. They should be on the noon train."

Jonathon stared at his mother, considering his response. He was well aware of the fact that his mother wanted him to court Caroline Collier, but he wasn't interested in such a commitment. Caroline was pretty and pleasant enough, but he'd felt no great attraction to her.

"Do you need me to send a car to collect them at the depot?"

Mother frowned. "Jonathon, I meant no such thing. Don't you want to see Caroline? Her mother told me Caroline spoke highly of you before they left and looked forward to seeing you again."

"Of course, Mother, we do get along, but you know how busy I am these days. I have much to do before the Assembly convenes this season."

"You are too busy for your own good, Jonathon."

"Father's businesses leave me little time for social affairs."

"Then I should invite the Colliers over for dinner. Surely you have time for dinner?"

He was caught. There was no way to avoid dinner. "I suppose I can make time for that. When are you thinking of having them?"

"I'll give them a day or so to rest from their travels first. Maybe later on this week?"

"Please let me know when the day and time is confirmed so I can put it on my schedule."

"I will." Mother's smile showed self-satisfaction that she had succeeded in her plans.

Jonathon put down the paper, then stood and crossed the room, bending over to give his mother a peck on the cheek. "You're incorrigible, Mother."

She gave him a playful push. "How will you ever find a wife if I don't help?"

Samuel approached with the coffee pot. "More coffee, sir?"

"Take the pot to my office, please."

"Yes, sir." Samuel bowed slightly, then retrieved Jonathon's cup and placed it on a tray with the pot, sugar bowl, and creamer before placing the tray on the dumbwaiter on the side of the room. He pulled the rope until the platform lifted and the rope was fully retrieved, then closed the door and turned to go upstairs.

Jonathon led the way through the grand foyer where the

morning sun splashed a kaleidoscope of color through the Tiffany stained glass accent window above the staircase onto the room below, competing with the rich Aubusson rug for attention. Samuel followed a few steps behind, and when they reached the tower office, he opened the dumbwaiter and retrieved the tray. Jonathon strode to the window facing the lake, looking out as Samuel poured him a fresh cup of coffee, then handed it to him.

"Thank you, Samuel."

Jonathon's gaze skimmed the panorama before him, hoping to see Miss Morgan down by the lake again. A few early morning strollers walked on the path behind the Assembly Hall, but the pretty photographer wasn't in view. Her absence was disappointing, and he hoped he hadn't been too inhospitable. Perhaps she believed he had been offended by her trespassing when he went down to meet her. How could he prove she was welcome to return? He couldn't very well go to her aunt's house and invite her, could he? An idea struck him.

He turned from the window. "Samuel, I'd like to put a bench down by the water. Would you please ask the gardener to move the one by the fountain to the water's edge? I'll buy a new one for the garden." Perhaps she would notice his gesture as an invitation and use the bench to balance her tripod.

"Yes, sir." Samuel bowed his head, then left.

Samuel, the dutiful servant, always did his bidding. Jonathon identified with the man, as he was also in servitude to his mother, and to his father as well, before he died. Jonathon was always the obedient, compliant child, the only son, and the one who would follow in his father's footsteps. He'd been given a year abroad after graduating from Yale but had to cut his trip short when his father suddenly grew ill. His death soon afterward had forced Jonathon into his role as head of the family businesses, a position for which he did not feel qualified.

He gazed up at the photo of his grandfather above the fireplace mantel. Jonathon was certain the man watched him at work because the eyes in the portrait followed him everywhere. "Grandfather, I don't know how I can ever live up to your reputation," Jonathon muttered. Especially when he wanted to choose his own future. Grandfather had been an entrepreneur. He had built his businesses and the town from the ground up. Jonathon's father had slipped into the position seemingly easy. But he'd had time to work alongside Grandfather and learn the business. Jonathon, on the other hand, had only recently graduated from college when Father died. If only he'd lived long enough to guide his only son.

He wondered why his father even sent him to college if all he was supposed to do when he graduated was run the family's businesses. He hadn't even studied business in college. Instead, he had studied history and received a Bachelor of Arts degree. During his short time in Europe, he'd relished seeing historic sites he'd only read about. Perhaps someday, he'd have time to return and spend more time there. He shook his head. When did his father ever have time for a vacation? Even in this peaceful setting by the lake, the man had worked non-stop, and Mother wondered if too much work had a part in his early death.

Jonathon sat behind his desk and reviewed his calendar for the day's tasks. A meeting with the planning committee of the Assembly was first on the list. The chairmanship of the committee had passed down to him along with his other responsibilities, and he hoped he could make this year's event as successful as those in the past. After the meeting, he planned to visit the mercantile to speak with the manager about the upcoming Christmas season. Afterwards, a board meeting at church, another position he'd inherited. Meetings all day. He exhaled a long sigh and steeled himself for a boring day as he gathered the notes he'd need for each meeting. He lifted his gaze to the ceiling. *Lord, please give me wisdom for each of these meetings.*

At the Assembly Hall, he was briefed on the agenda for the upcoming conference. Noted lecturers and educators were lined up to speak to the attendees coming from all over the country for enlightenment. Jonathon hoped he'd be able to hear some of them. He was reminded that he'd be expected to give a welcoming speech at the opening meeting. What on earth would he say beyond "Welcome to Springlake?" Perhaps Mother could help him write the speech. She'd attended every Assembly since she'd married Father, plus she was accustomed to addressing the women in her social club.

During the meeting, Jonathon kept his eyes focused on the lake behind the hall. No sign of Miss Morgan. Had she finished taking all the photographs she wanted?

The mercantile was busy, and Jonathon spent some time perusing the shelves until the manager was free to talk with him. They certainly carried a wide variety of goods, much more than he remembered. He strolled along the length of the glass-topped counter, checking to see what was inside, then almost bumped into a lady who was also looking into the counter.

"Excuse me," he said, his hand at the tip of his hat.

Loretta Morgan glanced up and her green eyes widened with recognition. "Oh! Mr. Townsend!" She touched the lady's elbow beside her. "Aunt Gertie, this is Jonathon Townsend. I met him yesterday by the lake."

The white-haired lady beside her wearing a broad-brimmed black straw hat and a black walking suit, looked over at him and smiled. She extended her gloved hand. "Good morning, Mr. Townsend. I haven't seen you since we returned to the cottage. I was so sorry to hear of your father's passing. How is your dear mother?"

"Thank you, Mrs. Ross. Mother is doing well. I'll tell her you asked. Perhaps you'd like to come by the house and see her." And bring your niece, he wanted to say. "I'm sure she would welcome your company."

"I will certainly do that." She turned to Loretta. "I see you've met my niece, Lettie Morgan."

"Lettie?" He faced her. "Didn't you say your name was Loretta?"

She blushed. "It's my formal name, yes, but my friends and family call me Lettie."

"Oh, I see." If only he could be considered part of her close circle familiar enough to call her Lettie as well. But this was just the second time he'd seen her, even though it seemed he'd known her longer.

A salesclerk walked up and cleared his throat. "Sorry to interrupt you, sir, but Mr. Franklin said he would be tied up for some time and asked if he could postpone your meeting."

"Of course. Can you ask him to drop by Magnolia Manor when he gets off work? He can telephone to let me know what time he'll be by."

The clerk's head bobbed. "Yes, sir. I will. Good day, sir." He nodded toward the women. "Please excuse me, ladies." Then he backed away and hurried out.

"We were just leaving, actually," Mrs. Ross said. "We didn't find what we were looking for."

He raised his eyebrows. "No? What, pray tell, if you don't mind?"

Lettie glanced at her aunt and answered. "A journal. For me. Auntie believes I should record my impressions about the photos I shoot."

"Excellent idea. That way, you can convey the feelings you have about the photograph when you take it. I can see how a journal would be of great benefit." He looked around. "And they don't have one here?" He needed to say "we," but didn't feel the store was his as much as it was those who ran it.

Both ladies shook their heads. "We asked the clerk and he pointed us in this direction, but we didn't find any," said Lettie.

"The gentleman said they might be sold out," added Mrs. Ross.

Jonathon rubbed his chin. "I would expect them to stock extra this time of year with so many coming for the Assembly. Most attendees would like to take notes during the presentations. I'll speak to the manager about it."

The ladies smiled, and Jonathon felt important being able to rectify the problem. For once, he liked having authority over the business. Hopefully, the manager would accept his recommendation.

The train whistle diverted his attention. Caroline would be on that train. He hadn't planned on running into her yet. But he had to pass by the depot on the way home, and if he saw her, he'd be expected to stop and speak. However, he had no reason to spend any more time in the mercantile.

He extended his arm. "Ladies, may I escort you out?"

"Thank you." Mrs. Ross took Lettie's arm and proceeded toward the front of the store. He opened the door for them and as they walked outside, Lettie gasped.

He glanced at her to see what had happened. "Is everything all right?"

She pointed down the street. "A carousel! I didn't know there was one in town!"

Indeed, the town merry-go-round was housed in a large circus-style tent only a short distance way. It'd been so long since he'd been on the merry-go-round, he'd forgotten it was there. Apparently, it hadn't been running when she and her aunt entered the mercantile or they would have heard the music. But with more visitors coming into town, Jonathon expected the amusement ride would get much busier.

"There was a delivery wagon blocking our view when we arrived earlier," Mrs. Ross said.

"So you like carousels?" Jonathon's spirit lifted at the delight on Lettie's face.

"Of course! Who doesn't? I've always loved to ride them!"

"Then you must!" He glanced to see if any carriages or wagons were coming, then motioned for them to cross the street. Lettie looked at him with wonder, but took her aunt's arm and accompanied Jonathon across, then over to the carousel.

"But is it running this time of day?" Lettie gazed at the unmoving merry-go-round.

"It runs when customers arrive." Jonathon signaled to an attendant sitting on one of the ornate benches of the ride. The man jumped to his feet and hurried over. "Yes, sir, Mr. Townsend. Would you like me to start her up?"

"Yes, please. These ladies would like a ride."

"I'm not certain I should ride the conveyance," Mrs. Ross said. "I'm afraid it might bring on one of my headaches."

Lettie took her aunt's hand. "Please, Aunt Gertie. It might be good for you too."

Mrs. Ross frowned. "I don't know. I might get dizzy."

"We won't go that fast, I promise. But if you'd prefer not to, that's your decision."

Mrs. Ross looked from the carousel to Lettie, then Jonathon. She blew out a breath. "All right. I'll give it a try. But don't expect me to climb up on one of those horses."

Jonathon smiled and led the ladies over. "Why don't you sit here?" He motioned to a stationary bench. "It has the least amount of movement." She complied, sitting stiffly with her purse set upon her lap.

"I want to ride the biggest, fastest animal here!" Miss Morgan hurried to the area where the animals would move up and down on poles.

"A horse or a tiger?" Jonathon asked.

She put her finger to her mouth as if in deep thought. Then she exclaimed, "Oh! That one! It's beautiful!"

She ran to the horse, truly one of the most attractive animals on the carousel, white with a gold-trimmed saddle and yellow and pink flowers accenting a blue sash painted on its side, a blue and pink harness painted on the head. The horse was poised as if running, adding to its exciting décor.

"Good choice. I believe you've chosen the fastest animal." Her enthusiasm was contagious, and he smiled as he joined her beside the horse. "May I give you a lift?" There was no way she could get on the large animal on her own.

She nodded, and he lifted her up on the saddle, a surge of energy coursing through him as his hands practically encircled her waist.

"I suppose I'll have to ride side-saddle, as I have no riding britches on today." She leaned over and patted the horse's head as if it were real.

"Have you ridden real horses?"

"Of course, though not often. We don't own any, so I've only ridden when I've visited friends who do. Actually, I'd love to ride more often." She glanced at him. "Which one will you ride?"

"Me? I thought I might need to help you hang on, but I see you're an accomplished equestrian. Why don't I ride this thoroughbred here beside you?" He laid his hand on a black horse, painted to look fierce.

"Perfect. Then we can race!"

Jonathon laughed aloud as he climbed onto the horse. He motioned to the attendant to start the carousel, then looked at Lettie Morgan sitting like an eager child beside him. "You're on!"

Chapter Three

Lettie couldn't remember when she'd had so much fun. She'd certainly misjudged Mr. Townsend, expecting him to be more stodgy and proper than to ride a carousel.

When the ride finally ended, no doubt a longer than normal ride by the signals Mr. Townsend had given the attendant, she was exhilarated as if she'd ridden a real horse. Poor Aunt Gertie, however, had not enjoyed the ride as much. In fact, both Lettie and Mr. Townsend had to help her to her feet and steady her as they disembarked the ride.

"Are you all right, Aunt Gertie?"

"I'll be fine, as long as I can find my balance again."

"May I drive you home? My car is right over there." Mr. Townsend nodded toward an exquisite Pierce Arrow, its shining garnet red finish accented by gleaming white sidewall tires. Lettie would love to ride in such a beautiful car.

"What a magnificent car!" Lettie couldn't contain her admiration.

"It's a bit ostentatious, I'm afraid, but Father insisted on buying it after his friend and fellow Yale classmate, President Taft bought one."

Lettie tried not to act surprised that the Townsend family had connections to the president. "Thank you, but we have

Auntie's car." She inwardly sighed and pointed to her aunt's green Model T not far from the Arrow.

"I see. Will she be able to drive it?"

Lettie laughed. "I do all the driving when I'm here. I enjoy it, and Auntie is happy to let me do it."

"Then may I start it for you?"

"That would be wonderful." The crank that started the car could sometimes be difficult, and Lettie was always grateful a man was around to help, especially since Aunt Gertie didn't have the strength for it. Lettie hoped her aunt would recover from the carousel ride soon, so she wouldn't feel so guilty about forcing her to participate.

After Mr. Townsend helped them into the car and Lettie had set the magneto to the starting position, he went to the front and turned the hand crank until the engine started. He smiled and brushed off his hands as he came back around to Lettie's side of the car. "There you go!" he said.

"Thank you so much. And especially for entertaining us today. I don't think I've had as much fun since I was a child!"

Mr. Townsend's smile made him even more handsome, a feat seemingly impossible. "You are quite welcome. We will have to do that again sometime."

Lettie's face flushed, as she'd like nothing more, but she didn't want to expect the impromptu experience to be repeated. She'd learned that getting her hopes up could lead to disappointment, and she hated to be disappointed. "You know, I'd absolutely love to photograph the carousel. I believe I'll come back another time and do just that."

A curious expression crossed his face, transforming the smile to a more polite, if not forced effort. Was he extending an invitation that she didn't answer? Or was he just being the well-mannered gentleman that he'd been trained to be?

It didn't matter. She had no expectations from him, and he certainly had none from her. She would only be there a short time anyway, then she'd be gone, and he'd carry on with running the town.

When Jonathon returned home later, his mother met him in the foyer, worry creasing her face.

"Jonathon! Something terrible has happened!"

Jonathon handed his hat to Samuel, then placed his hands on his mother's shoulders. "Mother, what?" The last time he'd seen his normally calm mother upset was when he'd returned home after Father's heart attack.

"Jonathon, the train was robbed!"

"Robbed? Where?"

"Between Jacksonville and Chattahoochee. The Colliers were on that train. They are quite upset."

"Was anyone hurt?"

Mother put her hand over her heart. "No, thank God. But the robber had a gun and threatened to shoot anyone who tried to stop him. Oh, Jonathon, what are we going to do?"

We? What she meant was what was *he* going to do. As one of the railroad owners, he was responsible for the safety of the passengers.

"I'll have to make some calls. I need to call the other owners, Mr. Steadman and Mr. Bishop. And I'll have to call the Pinkerton agency too. I'm sure they'll want to interview the passengers involved. Was much taken?"

"Every bit of cash they carried and jewelry they wore. Fortunately, the rest of their valuables were packed in their luggage in the baggage car."

Some consolation, but he knew how the ladies liked to flaunt their expensive jewelry. "Does anyone know where the thief went?"

Mother shook her head. "No, Dorothy and I didn't discuss that. She was so distraught, the poor woman."

"And Caroline? How is she?"

Mother shrugged. "I don't know. Dorothy said they were all upset. Dear, what can we do?"

"We can tell them we will do all we can to apprehend the thief and restore their losses." Hopefully, that answer would pacify the passengers.

"I just can't believe someone would do such a thing these days. Why, we're civilized here in Florida! We don't live out west where all those wild outlaws are, where things such as this happen."

"I agree, Mother. Well, please excuse me. I need to get right on this."

He turned on his heel and trotted upstairs to the office. Picking up the telephone receiver, he reached the operator and asked her to connect him with his partners. If the news about the robbery hadn't reached the whole town by now, he was sure it would be by the time Florence, the town operator, finished connecting all his calls. He hated the fact that she probably heard much of his conversation, even though she wasn't supposed to listen in. But he also knew Florence was a source of news as much as the newspaper was. They might as well have a town crier.

This turn of events couldn't have come at a worse time. People were arriving every day for the Assembly, and news of a train robbery could scare would-be attendees away. Not to mention the complaints that would inevitably be lodged against the railroad. He knew how these things worked—give people a reason to criticize, and they'd come up with a multitude of grievances.

Alarm raced through him. Had any of the renowned faculty been on the train? The burden of responsibility weighed on him like a sack of bricks. His shoulders sagged, and he propped his elbows on his desk, holding his face with his hands. *Lord, I can't do this. This problem is too much, too large for me to handle.*

Someone cleared his throat. Jonathon looked up to see Samuel standing in front of the desk. "Sorry to interrupt you, sir."

"That's all right, Samuel. What do you need?"

"I'm here to see what *you* need, sir. Is there anything I can do to help?"

Jonathon stared at the white-haired elderly gentleman who had served his family since before Jonathon was born. "Thank you, Samuel. Since you've been here since Grandfather was alive, you'd know what he would do. What would Father do? They're not here to tell me."

Samuel nodded, a faint glimmer of a smile on his face. "I can't tell you exactly what they'd do, sir. But one thing I do know for sure." He motioned to the old Bible sitting on the corner of the desk, the one that had always sat there. "I know both your father and your grandfather would open that book to look for answers. Maybe you can find some in there too."

Jonathon reached for the Holy Book, its leather cracked and worn, its pages yellowed. When was the last time it had been opened? Probably when Father was alive, because Jonathon hadn't. A tinge of guilt pierced his heart. He hadn't even thought about it and had become so familiar with it being on the desk, it might as well have been a desk accessory. But where in the Bible did it talk about railroads and train robbers?

He looked up at Samuel again. "I suppose it can't hurt, can it?"

Samuel smiled with a twinkle in his eye. "No sir, it can't hurt."

Samuel left the room, and Jonathon opened the Bible to the center where it fell open in the book of Psalms. He read the words of David, the shepherd-boy turned king, and noticed a pattern. Many times, the chapter began with David calling out to God for help, but by the end of the chapter David was praising God by saying things like "the Lord is a shield, a stronghold, a refuge." He said the Lord was his counselor who instructed him in the way he should go. After reading a while, he closed the book, knowing he wasn't alone, and that the same God his father and grandfather had believed in was there for him too and would help him know what to do.

He picked up a pen and wrote on a blank sheet of paper, making a list of things that needed to be done. When he finished noting everything he could think of, he went back over the list and assigned a priority number. Afterwards, he reviewed the list and knew exactly what he needed to do in what order. Leaning back in the chair, he blew out a deep breath. He would handle one thing at a time, and his first order of business was to go to the telegraph office and send a message to William Rogers, one of his partners in the railroad.

Mr. Rogers lived in Pensacola, and Jonathon decided it would be best and more private to send a telegram. He'd also be spared the man's temper. But he could just imagine the man's red face and hear his bellowing when the telegram arrived. Of course, the phone service between Springlake and Pensacola was not very reliable, and this way, Florence wouldn't have to hear their private conversation. While he was at the telegraph office, he'd send one to the Pinkerton Agency and apprise them of the situation. The sooner, the better. Who knew how far away the robber had gotten by now? James Stanley, who owned the bank, was the other partner. He lived in town, and Jonathon could go see him in person, even though it was quite possible word of the robbery had reached him already.

Jonathon pulled on his jacket, grabbed the list, folded it, and stuck it in his inside pocket. He snatched his hat off the hall tree as he hurried out, passing Samuel on the way. "Please tell Mother I must go to town."

He hopped in the Pierce-Arrow for the short ride. Ahead, the hotel's verandas were full of ladies and gentlemen enjoying the mild Florida weather. Many, he assumed, had just arrived. Others strolled along the lake, waving to him as he passed. He nodded, wondering how many of them had been victims of the train robbery.

As he turned toward town, a small group gathered around someone in the hotel's lawn caught his eye. One of the presenters or performers, no doubt. He cringed at the thought that these dignitaries had been subjected to such humiliation on his train. His train. At one time, the concept of owning the railroad had appeared to be an honor. Right now, though, he'd just as soon that responsibility belonged to someone else.

He pulled up in front of the First National Bank of Springlake and hopped out. Casting a glance at the bank tellers inside, he strode to the office of James Stanley and knocked.

"Come in," the bank president answered.

Jonathon stepped inside and removed his hat. Mr. Stanley's vest strained as he leaned back in his chair and eyed Jonathon, his bushy white eyebrows raised. "Been expecting you." He pointed to the chair across the desk from him.

"Yes, sir. I assume you heard about the robbery." Jonathon sat, holding his hat on his knee.

"I did. We don't need this kind of trouble. Bad news travels fast, and we don't want this incident to spoil this year's attendance to the Assembly." The banker steepled his fingers, frowning.

Jonathon swallowed. "No, sir. We don't."

"So what are we going to do about it? Do we know who this thief is or where he came from?"

"No. What have you heard?" Jonathon was certain the bank's customers had been buzzing about the incident.

"You know how rumors are—said the man walked through the car demanding money and jewels, waving a gun. No one saw him get off the train when they arrived at the last stop, so they're guessing he jumped from the train when it slowed down."

"I'm going to telegraph the Pinkertons as soon as I leave here," Jonathon said, trying to sound as if he knew what to do.

"What about William? Does he know?"

"I doubt it, but I'm going to send him a telegraph too." The least Jonathon could do was send messages.

Mr. Stanley tapped his fingers on the desk. "We need to get this man. I don't want my customers to think there's a robber on the loose. What's to keep him from showing up here at the bank?"

Jonathon shook his head. "Surely he wouldn't. When I telegraph the Pinkertons, I'll ask for some extra security until he's caught. We might need it until the Assembly is over as well."

"Good idea. Sheriff Williams doesn't have enough help to devote to the bank as well as the Assembly. But we have a lot of wealthy guests in town, many who would like to keep their valuables here in the meantime. They must be assured their valuables will be safe."

"I agree. I'll notify the insurance company too."

Mr. Stanley grimaced. "Hope those people are honest about what was taken. But there's no way to verify, I guess."

Jonathon stood. "I better get over to the telegraph office now. We can't afford to waste any time."

Stanley nodded. "You go along, then. Keep me abreast of anything you find out, and I'll do the same."

Jonathon replaced his bowler, nodded, then let himself out.

The good thing about having the telegraph office inside the mercantile meant there was a greater regard for confidentiality. Homer, the telegraph operator, had worked for the Townsend family for years and could be trusted to be discreet. Jonathon wrote out the messages Homer was to send, then handed them over. The man's eyes bugged out as he read the messages. He glanced up at Jonathon, then his fingers went to work sending the telegraphs. Jonathon waited, looking around the store and wondering who else had heard about the robbery so far. It wouldn't take long for word to travel through their small town.

Once the Pinkertons were in town, they'd question everyone who was on the train. But Jonathon wanted to speak to someone who had witnessed it too. Should he conduct his own investigation or let the Pinkertons handle it all? After all, they wouldn't be here for days. Caroline. He could visit her and her mother and hear their version of what happened. Looked like he'd have to see her before Mother's scheduled dinner.

On the way home, he stopped at his house to let Mother know he was planning to visit the Colliers. Then he placed a call to their house to see if it was a good time for him to come by.

Caroline answered the phone. "Hello?"

"Caroline, it's Jonathon. Welcome back."

"Oh, Jonathon. I'm so glad to be back, especially after that horrid experience on the train!"

"I heard. I'm very sorry you had to endure that. Do you think I might drop by and talk to you about it, or are you too tired for visitors?"

"No, please come by. Mother's resting, but I'm much better, now that we're here. I'd love to see you, Jonathon. It's been so long."

Jonathon drew in a breath. He knew she expected his attention, but he was afraid she expected more than that. He wasn't ready to court her yet. They'd known each other for years, and it seemed their mothers wanted them to marry someday. But Caroline felt more like a sister to him.

Well, he had to go see her, regardless of anyone's expectations. This visit was pure business, though, whether anyone else realized it or not.

Chapter Four

Caroline's face beamed when she opened the door. "I'm so glad to see you, Jonathon!"

"Is Jonathon here?" The voice of Caroline's younger sister Constance rang out behind her. As he stepped into the foyer, Constance hurried to greet him. She stopped short with a glance from Caroline, then dipped a quick curtsy. "Hello, Jonathon." Constance's resemblance to her sister was indisputable, as both had fair skin, hazel eyes, chestnut brown hair, and a slightly turned-up nose. Teenage Constance's hair was pulled back into a braid with a large bow tied to it, though, while Caroline's hair was in the pompadour style.

"Hello, Caroline. And Constance." He nodded a bow to each of them, producing a rosy hue in Constance's face. Jonathon was well aware of the adoration Constance had always had for him, as she hung onto his every word and couldn't keep her eyes off him. Her presence used to make him uncomfortable, but he had gotten used to her behavior.

Caroline extended her hand. "Please. Come into the parlor. Coffee or tea?"

"Whatever you have available will be fine."

He followed Caroline into the parlor where Mrs. Collier rose to greet him. "Jonathon. You look well."

"As do you, Mrs. Collier." She motioned to a chair and

he took it. A maid came in carrying a tray with cookies and two gleaming silver pitchers, setting it down on the serving cart. She glanced at Jonathon.

"I'll have coffee, thank you."

The maid poured the coffee and handed him a cup and saucer, then poured tea for Mrs. Collier and Caroline. Constance grabbed a napkin and two cookies, then sat down on the ottoman nearest Jonathon.

Jonathon cleared his throat. "Well, first I'd like to apologize to you all for the frightening experience you had today. I'm so sorry for your inconvenience."

"Thank you, Jonathon. It was a truly terrifying experience," Mrs. Collier said, while her daughters bobbed their heads in agreement.

"Do you mind telling me the details of the robbery? The Pinkertons are coming tomorrow to investigate, but I'd like to hear firsthand what happened."

All three women began talking at once, and he held up his hands in surrender. They silenced, then Mrs. Collier nodded to Caroline. "You go ahead and tell the story, Caroline."

Caroline cast an anxious glance toward her mother. "Well, we'd been out of Jacksonville a while and everyone had settled into their seats. A few people had dozed off, and not many people were talking. Then we heard a woman scream, and everyone sat up and looked around. Right after that, a man came into the car, waving a gun and demanding everyone to stay quiet and hand over all our money and jewels." She shuddered and paused to take a sip from her cup. "He went all the way through the car and threatened to shoot anyone who moved. One of the men stood up and said, 'Listen now. You can't do this,' and the robber held the gun up to the man's face and said he'd kill him if he didn't sit down and shut up.'"

"That man was Baxter Honeywell, one of the Assembly presenters," Mrs. Collier said.

Jonathon cringed, hearing what he'd dreaded.

"I was so afraid the robber would shoot him, I held my breath. In fact, I think I held my breath the whole time the thief was in the car," Mrs. Collier continued.

"So where did he go when he left?" Jonathon said.

"He left our car, and we heard another woman scream, then he was gone."

"Do you know what other performers were on the train?"

"Miss Helene Dupont. She was in her pullman car during the robbery but ran into the robber when she opened the door to step out. He jerked off the necklace she was wearing, then ran out the back of the car, she said."

"And then he jumped off the train!" Constance chimed in.

"Did anyone see him do that?"

Their heads nodded. "Several said they saw him jump when the train slowed down."

"What did he look like?"

"We couldn't see his face because he wore a neckerchief over his face plus a hat. He had on a long, loose overcoat and wore gloves. You couldn't tell much about him, but he seemed a quite tall. Of course, we were sitting down, so maybe he looked tall because we were looking up."

Jonathon shook his head. "That's not much to go on. But he had to have bought a ticket to travel. I wonder if anyone recognized him from boarding?"

"Nobody said they'd ever seen him before," Constance said. "Are you going to catch him?"

"Someone will, but probably not me." Jonathon gave her a slight smile. "But don't worry, we'll have the experts track him down."

"I hope they find him soon, before he can rob more innocent people," Mrs. Collier said.

"The insurance company will be contacting you, but do you mind telling me what he took from you?"

"I don't mind," Mrs. Collier said. "He took my ruby

brooch and gold bracelet I was wearing. I had to give it to him because I was afraid he would jerk it off. He also took Caroline's pearl necklace and Constance's cameo we bought in Europe."

Jonathon shook his head. "I'm so sorry."

"I loved that cameo." Constance stuck out her lips and tears gathered in the corner of her eyes. Mrs. Collier reached out and patted her hand.

"Did he also take any money from you?"

Mrs. Collier nodded. "Yes, I had about two hundred dollars in my purse. Thankfully, the rest of our jewelry and money was packed in our valise which was beneath our seat. I didn't even think to take it out, and the robber didn't seem to notice it either. Maybe he was in too big a hurry to search under the seats, especially since he got so much from our persons. But I'm thankful he didn't."

"Yes, that's a blessing," he said. "I'm sorry to make you relive that experience, but I must find out all I can so we can apprehend the man." He held out his cup when Mrs. Collier offered the pot to him.

"We understand." Mrs. Collier said.

"I had hoped to hear about your cruise to Europe instead, but this problem interfered. I trust the rest of your trip was enjoyable?"

"It was grand!" Constance declared.

Caroline cut her eyes to her sister. "Yes, it was very nice. The Baltic is a very elegant ship."

"And it's the fastest and the biggest ship in the whole world!" Constance added.

Caroline glanced away from her sister and rolled her eyes.

The clock in the parlor struck three, and Jonathon put his coffee cup and saucer down, then stood. "Please excuse me, I must go. I'm afraid I'll have to hear about the rest of your trip when you come to dinner tomorrow night."

"Thank you for coming by, Jonathon," Mrs. Collier said.

"I'll walk you out," Caroline said, glaring at Constance as if daring her to follow.

Jonathon couldn't wait to get outside and gave Caroline a brief goodbye before going out. She stood in the door, and he sensed her watch him to his car. Before he cranked the car, he gave her a wave, hoping she'd be satisfied with his meager gesture.

"The program for this year's Assembly has some very interesting features," Aunt Gertie said. "Everything from speakers to musicians to actors."

Aunt Gertie studied the Springlake Beacon, the local newspaper, as she lounged in the chaise and sipped tea on the sun porch on the side of her house. A cool afternoon breeze mingled with the warmth of the sun, typical of a Florida autumn day.

"Oh? Who? I heard The Jubilee Singers from Fisk University would be here. They're supposed to be very good."

"Yes, they are. I've seen them once before and thoroughly enjoyed their style of singing spirituals. But there's also going to be an opera singer as well...Eloise Bristol from England."

"Hmm. What a contrast." Lettie poured herself a cup of tea from the pitcher on the tray, picking up a tea cake to place beside the cup on the saucer.

"Yes, it is. And there's also going to be a string quartet."

Lettie settled into a wicker chair and took a bite of the cookie. "Who are the speakers? Are they all politicians and preachers?"

Aunt Gertie raised her eyebrows at Lettie. "Not all, but yes, some are. However, Jane Adams will be here talking about her work with the poor in Chicago. And Baxter

Honeywell, the Englishman. I understand he's quite an orator."

"I wish I could have heard Mark Twain," Lettie said. "Father and Mother said he was quite enjoyable."

"Yes, he was, but unfortunately, he passed away earlier this year. He was such a humorous man, poking fun at everything and everyone. Oh, but I see Opie Read will be here. He's in semi-retirement and doesn't travel much anymore, but he's almost as enjoyable as Mr. Twain was. And he's written over sixty books!"

"He's almost as prolific as you are, Aunt Gertie!"

Aunt Gertie chuckled. "I'm afraid he's got me beat, Lettie. I've only written half that many."

Lettie leaned over toward her aunt. "Does the paper say which actors will be here?"

"Helene Dupont. She's quite talented and has performed a number of roles around the country as well as Europe. And she can sing as well."

"Now that's one thing I'd definitely like to see. I get a little bored with too many lectures."

Aunt Gertie's smile was negligible. "I must admit, sometimes I do too."

Lettie glanced out the room toward the lake, just in time to see Jonathon Townsend's car pass by. Warmth coursed through her as she recalled the carousel ride, especially when he lifted her onto the horse.

"I suppose Mr. Townsend is involved with the Assembly too."

"Definitely. He'll introduce the president of the Assembly on the first day, plus of course, he's involved in the whole affair as well, such as procuring the performers."

"Auntie, if you don't need me for a while, I think I'll go over to the little library by the lake. I'd like to see if they have any books on birds and find out more about the ones I've been photographing."

"You go on. I'll just rest a bit, then when you get back,

we can talk about my next book."

Lettie finished her cookie, then put down her teacup on the tray. She grabbed the jacket of her walking suit and put it on, studying her reflection in the mirror of the hall tree as she repinned an escaped lock back into her upswept hair. She secured her hat, then pulled on her gloves. Grabbing her camera equipment, she stepped outside.

A ripple of excitement coursed through her at the sight of Jonathon Townsend's car parked in front of a house two doors down. Who lived there? She started to go back inside and ask her aunt but decided against it. She shouldn't be so nosy. She crossed the lane and over to the path beside the lake. A number of people were taking an afternoon stroll, more than she'd seen since arriving at Springlake, and they seemed to be having lively conversations. Obviously, they were in town for the Assembly. She nodded to others as they passed, then stopped to capture a picture of the entire waterfront scene. Although she preferred taking photos of nature, people could also be good subjects, especially if she caught them off-guard and not posing.

Two women in huge hats topped with masses of flowers walked beside each other, their wide brims touching each time one leaned toward the other to chat. Lettie would stick to her straw boater which was much more practical. However, the ladies would make an interesting picture. She turned on the camera and held it eye-level, then pushed the shutter. Perhaps she should have introduced herself to them first, but they had passed without noticing her, so caught up in their conversation.

After taking several pictures, Lettie walked to the little white frame building that housed the Springlake Library. The quaint, miniature library was so unique and cozy, drastically different from the huge library she'd seen in New York City. In fact, this one could fit inside the city library several times. Reminding her of a dollhouse, the building was barely large enough to house a few hundred books. A pleasant-faced woman with neat brown hair pulled into a bun at her neck, sat behind a table.

She smiled at Lettie. "Good afternoon. May I help you find something?"

Lettie returned her smile. "Yes, please. Do you have any books about birds?"

"Yes, as a matter of fact." She rose from her chair and walked toward a section of shelves. Motioning to Lettie, she said, "Here's our selection on this shelf. Perhaps you can find something you're looking for."

Lettie walked over and scanned the shelf. She picked up a book and flipped through it, disappointed by the lack of pictures. She chose another and found a few sketches. Sighing, she put the book back on the shelf.

"Oh, ma'am, I forgot! We have four volumes of the Audubon book, *Birds of America*. Silly me, we keep them over there in a special cabinet. You know, they're fairly scarce."

Lettie followed the woman over to a glass case she opened. "Thank you."

"They're heavy books, so if you'd like to take one over to that little table, it would be easier to look at."

Lettie carried one of the volumes to a table by the window and opened it. The colors of the birds were wonderful, and she turned each page carefully, taking in the detail. When she found the pictures of waterfowl, she stopped, amazed at the realism in the pictures. The birds were posed, as if modeling for the picture. How could she get the birds she photographed to be so still?

"Do you have something I can write on? I'd like to jot down the names of the birds I've seen here on the lake, but I forgot to bring any paper."

"Of course. Looks like we're both being forgetful today. Guess it's with all that talk about the train robbery, I'm a bit distracted." The woman retrieved a piece of paper and a pencil, then brought it to Lettie.

"Train robbery? Where? When?"

"You haven't heard? My goodness. Our train was robbed this morning on its way here from Jacksonville."

Lettie's pulse quickened. "Oh my. Were any of the Springlake passengers robbed?"

The woman's head bobbed. "Yes, bless their hearts. He took all their jewelry and money. They were terrified."

"I imagine so. Was anyone hurt?"

"I don't think so. They said he waved a gun around and threatened to shoot anyone who didn't cooperate." She leaned forward and lowered her voice. "I heard some of the performers for the Assembly were onboard."

"Oh dear. That's terrible." Lettie recalled the people Aunt Gertie had talked about. "I hope they're still able to perform."

"I hope so, too."

Lettie spent some time looking at the book and writing down the names of the birds she recognized from the lake, all the while thinking about the train robbery. When she finished with the book, she stood. "Thank you for your help. I believe I've found all I need for now."

"You come back any time, that is, when we're open. The books will still be here."

Lettie left the library and headed back to Aunt Gertie's house. Had she heard about the robbery yet? Did she know anyone who had been robbed?

The Pierce Arrow was still parked in the same spot. As Lettie passed by, the front door of the house opened, and Jonathon Townsend came out. A pretty brunette stood in the doorway, smiling as he walked toward his car. He looked back and waved, and the girl did too. Then he cranked the engine and climbed in. Lettie quickly faced away, hoping they didn't see her watching. She increased her pace, trying to be invisible.

"Miss Morgan!"

Lettie halted, her heart skipping a beat as she turned

toward the voice coming from the car. Jonathon Townsend flashed a smile at her.

"Can I give you a ride somewhere?"

She shook her head, perhaps too much. "No, thank you. I'm going to my aunt's house. It's just ahead."

He glanced at Aunt Gertie's house. "Yes, I see."

What should she say? He was still there. "Would you like to stop in for a moment? I'm sure Aunt Gertie would like to see you." Would she? Aunt Gertie wasn't a stickler for protocol, but did she care if Mr. Townsend dropped by unannounced? Hopefully, she wouldn't mind, if by chance he did accept.

"Yes, I would. For just a moment." He leaned over and opened the car door. "Get in. I can take you the rest of the way."

It was silly of course, but the excitement of the opportunity overtook her reason, so she slid into the seat beside him. He pulled up to the front of Aunt Gertie's house and stopped. Lettie waited for him to come around to open the door, then accepted his hand to get out.

"Let me tell Aunt Gertie you're here, in case she's indisposed."

"I'll wait." He walked her to the front door, and she slipped inside.

Aunt Gertie had dozed off on the porch as Lettie suspected. She gently shook her aunt's shoulder.

"Aunt Gertie. We have company."

Her aunt's eyes fluttered open. "We do?" She glanced from side to side. "Where?"

"At the door. It's Mr. Townsend. May I invite him in?"

Aunt Gertie sat up. "Of course. I'll set some water on for tea."

"I don't think he'll be here that long."

"Oh? Well, don't keep him waiting."

"Aunt Gertie. Who lives two doors down in the two-story house with the cupola?"

"Hmm? Oh, that's the Collier house. They should be back soon for the season. Why?"

"Oh nothing. I just wondered." So that's where the future Mrs. Townsend lived. "I better go let Mr. Townsend in."

Lettie returned to the door and admitted Jonathon, her enthusiasm at his visit diminished. "Auntie is in the sunroom." She motioned to the open doorway leading to the room.

Mr. Townsend removed his hat and followed her direction. He stepped into the sunroom and smiled at Aunt Gertie. "Good afternoon, Mrs. Ross."

"Good afternoon, Jonathon." She motioned to a chair. "Won't you have a seat?"

"Thank you, but I can't stay long, I'm afraid."

Lettie reflected on how long his car had been parked in front of the Collier house. Apparently, he didn't mind staying longer at Caroline Collier's house.

Chapter Five

"I just stopped by to see how you're feeling and if you've recuperated from the carousel ride." Jonathon rotated his hat in his hands, aware that Lettie Morgan eyed him curiously.

"I'm fine, thank you." Mrs. Ross waved him off. "I don't expect I'll be taking any more carousel rides, though. I have enough headaches as it is."

Jonathon glanced at the attractive Miss Morgan, who plopped down on the settee across from him. Was she irritated with him? Or did he expect it because so many others were upset with him right now?

"I heard the train was robbed today," Miss Morgan said. Her tone was flat, but harbored accusation. Or had he assumed guilt for the incident?

Her aunt's eyes widened, and her hand went to her chest. "No!" she looked from Miss Morgan to Jonathon. "Is that true?"

Jonathon's face heated. Did he have to go through this again? Yes, and probably many more times. "Yes, unfortunately, it's true. A gunman held up the passengers between Jacksonville and here."

"Oh my? Was anyone hurt?"

"No, just frightened." He glanced at Miss Morgan for a reaction, but she only stared at him.

"Well, I should think so," Mrs. Ross said.

"Have they caught the robber yet?" Miss Morgan had a way of being direct, but he liked that. At least she said what she meant.

He shook his head. "Not yet."

Miss Morgan leaned forward. "What did he look like? Where did he get off?" The woman should be a reporter.

"No one has given much of a description, from what I know. Just a man with a long coat, a scarf covering his face and wearing a hat. And carrying a gun. Someone said they saw him jump off the train when it slowed down at Chattahoochee."

"Jumped? Seems like he'd get hurt."

"I guess if the train was moving slowly enough, which it would be when approaching a station, he could manage if he knew how to land correctly." She was asking him all the questions he'd asked himself. How could he give her answers when he didn't know anything? "The Pinkertons should be able to get to the bottom of all this when they arrive."

"The lady at the library said some of the Assembly dignitaries were on the train at the time too. I wonder how they're taking it."

Jonathon's stomach clenched with the unpleasant task of apologizing to the special guests for their inconvenience. Yet he knew it was something he had to do.

"I'm about to find out. I'm going to the hotel when I leave here. I hope they won't be too put off by the experience." He stood. This impulsive visit was not the right time for a social call. And the reception had not been what he'd hoped for either. At least not from Miss Morgan. "If you ladies will excuse me, I must go."

Miss Morgan stood as well. "I'll show you to the door." Was she anxious for him to leave?

"Goodbye, Jonathon. Thank you for stopping by. I'm sure the robber will be caught soon," Aunt Gertie said, standing to bid him goodbye.

At the door, he paused to attempt more pleasant conversation with Miss Morgan. "Have you taken any more pictures?"

She nodded and allowed a smile to turn her lips up. "Yes, today, I took a few before I went to the library. I even took pictures of some of the guests."

"And I thought you were only interested in photographing nature, birds in particular."

Her eyes sparkled as she released a smile. "If you saw the people whose pictures I took, you'd understand what unique specimens they are."

Jonathon laughed. "I'm sure you're right about that. The Assembly attracts many different varieties of 'birds.'"

His visit to Mrs. Ross's house had been short, but even with the friction, more refreshing than the time spent at the Collier house, as no one at the Ross cottage expected anything from him. But now it was time to go see the presenters who'd been on the train. He couldn't delay the task any longer.

He drove around the lake to the hotel and parked in front, gaining the attention of guests on the veranda and in the yard. They all smiled and nodded as he walked across the sidewalk to the front door, tipping his hat in return. At the reception desk, he inquired about who had checked in that day. The clerk was more than happy to oblige him and turned the guest register around so Jonathon could read it.

Miss Dupont and Mr. Honeywell were the only two presenters who had arrived that day, but several other guests had arrived with them. Jonathon asked where he might find the two notable guests so he could meet with them privately. He told the clerk to ask the manager to announce a meeting with the rest of the hotel guests afterwards. He found Miss Dupont seated on the veranda with a group gathered around her as she fanned herself with an elaborate silk fan.

"In my last performance in Paris, the audience gave me

three standing ovations!" She raised three fingers. "Three! They *loved* me!"

Oohs and aahs responded from the ogling group. Some even clapped. Jonathon stood outside the circle observing the actress. The statuesque woman had charcoal black hair barely visible under an oversized hat with an ostrich plume that danced as she gestured excessively with her hands. Her multi-layered lace dress was a bit too revealing in his opinion, but fortunately, she wore a silk kimono-type shawl loosely over it. She caught his eye and grinned.

"Who is this handsome young man? Are you one of my fans?"

Jonathon's face burned as he stepped forward. "Please excuse the interruption. My name is Jonathon Townsend. I'm the chairman of the Assembly, and I'd like to talk to you about the train robbery today. I understand you encountered the robber."

Miss Dupont's hand flew to her chest and she threw her head back as if she'd been shot. "Oh my! It was the most frightful experience of my life! I thought he was going to kill me!"

"I'm very sorry about your experience, Miss Dupont."

She shook her head, casting her eyes downward. "It was truly terrible indeed."

"Might I ask if you got a good look at the robber?"

"Got a good look? My heavens, I was face-to-face with him when I walked out of my room! I can barely recall anything but the evil in his eyes when he aimed the gun at me. I was terrified! Then, he jerked my diamond necklace off and stuffed it in his pocket before he ran out the back of the car."

"And did you see where he went after that?"

She nodded. "I looked out the window and saw him leap from the train! He rolled over and then the train had gone too far for me to see anymore."

"I apologize for the unfortunate incident. The railroad's

insurance company will be in touch with you about your loss. I hope the remainder of your visit here in Springlake will be much more pleasant and will somewhat make up for your distress."

"Thank you, dear sir. This is a lovely place, and I'm sure I will enjoy it here."

"Yes, it is. And I look forward to seeing your performances, as do all of these people." He swept his arm to include the circle of those standing around them.

She beamed at the compliment.

Jonathon stepped back. "Please excuse me." He walked away with the impression she was always performing. Truly, she craved the attention, but he, for one, wasn't attracted to her brazen, unsophisticated behavior.

Baxter Honeywell's accent revealed his identity where he sat in a large wicker chair around the opposite side of the hotel with several men standing nearby. His foot was crossed over his knee, and he held a smoking cigar in his long, thin fingers. He was dressed in an ivory linen suit with a straw boater looking as if he were in the tropics during the summer. But many northerners assumed any place in the south was appropriate for summer wear year-round. Mr. Honeywell had a sleek black moustache waxed to a point on each end and with a matching black goatee.

As Jonathon approached, he waved an ivory-handled cane toward him. "Won't you join us, sir?"

Jonathon tipped his hat. "Good afternoon. My name is Jonathon Townsend." He extended his hand.

"Ah, yes, I've heard of you." Honeywell shook hands. "You're the man in charge, I understand."

"Of some things, yes, the Assembly for one. I've come to apologize to you for your unfortunate incident today."

"Yes, well. That's very gracious of you, but I hardly think it was your fault." He drew on the cigar and blew smoke toward Jonathon.

"Perhaps not, but I hate for our guests to be

inconvenienced or disillusioned with our event."

"Mr. Townsend, you mustn't trouble yourself. The incident is over, and the thief is long gone into the annals of history."

"Would you mind telling me what you remember about it?"

"The bloke stormed into our car and demanded our valuables at gunpoint. He took what he wanted then left."

"Mr. Honeywell stood up to him. Almost got killed for it too!" one of the men nearby said.

Honeywell waved with his cigar hand. "I supposed I thought I could talk some sense into him. That was a foolhardy thing to do. When he threatened to shoot me, my courage receded quickly." He laughed, and the other men joined him.

"What else do you remember about him? Anything special about how he looked?"

"No. Poor dresser. Big sloppy overcoat, ugly fedora. Couldn't see his face for the kerchief tied around it."

"Did you happen to see his hair color or remember his eyes?"

"Hmm. I think his hair was brown, what I could see of it. Eyes? Beady, that's all."

"And did you see him get off the train?"

"Someone said he jumped. Didn't actually see it myself."

"That seems to be the general belief." Jonathon tipped his hat. "I'll be seeing you again soon, sir. Let me know if there's anything I can do for you."

"Thank you, Mr. Townsend."

Jonathon went back inside where the manager was waiting at the front desk, hair parted down the middle and slicked down. "Please announce to your guests that due to the inconvenience they suffered today, their evening meal will be compliments of the house."

The man's eyes widened. "Excuse me, sir. We can't

afford to do that."

"Perhaps not, but I can. Just let them believe the hotel is doing it, not me. Do I have your word?"

"Yes, sir! I'll make the announcement straight away!"

Jonathon nodded, then went back to his car. As he drove away, he saw the hotel manager step outside and ask for everyone's attention.

The first two detectives from The Pinkerton Agency arrived at the Townsend house two days later. Samuel admitted them, then rang upstairs on the intercom to alert Jonathon of their presence. He trotted down the stairs and invited them to join him in his office, aware that his father would have had the butler lead them up instead. But Jonathon didn't mind the exercise after sitting at his desk so long. After all, he was still young and in good health.

Jonathon asked Samuel to bring them coffee, then motioned for them to follow him up the stairs. Thomas Butler and Henry Jones were dressed in similar fashion, brown tweed suits and black derby hats. They took the seats offered, removed their hats, and began the investigation without any pleasantries. Jonathon noted how even their mannerisms were similar as if they were twins, although they didn't look alike with Mr. Butler being the older one, his hair and mustache streaked with gray. He was also heavier and taller than Mr. Jones, who stood about a foot shorter. As expected, they asked the same questions Jonathon had asked about the robbery. Mr. Butler seemed to be in charge, as he asked the most questions while Mr. Jones took notes and nodded.

Samuel served the men coffee which they gulped down, obviously in a hurry to stick to business.

"Isn't it possible that the thief got off at the next stop and didn't jump off?" Mr. Butler posed the question.

"I suppose it is possible, yes, if he was first to disembark or even last, so as not to be detected. However, if that's the case, those who saw him jump weren't telling the truth."

Mr. Butler nodded. "True, but we've found that in the retelling of an exciting story, people often add their own details. Their memory gets blurred, you might say."

Jonathon couldn't imagine how anyone would add that detail, but the consensus from those he'd spoken to was that the man indeed had jumped from the train. He couldn't remember who had told him they actually witnessed the man exiting the train in such a way. Besides, why would they lie about it?

"And the description—tall, long brown coat, kerchief covering face, black hat—pretty standard." Mr. Jones snapped his notebook closed. "We'll talk to the passengers and see what else we can find out."

They stood, and Jonathon did the same, feeling a bit inept for not learning more about the incident. However, these men had experience solving crimes, and he didn't. At least he could be confident they'd get to the bottom of it soon, and things could return to normal.

"Thank you, Mr. Townsend." Mr. Butler extended his hand. "If you could direct us to the hotel? We'll be staying there, so we should be able to interview the guests involved. If you know of anyone else onboard, please let us know so we may speak to them too."

"Mrs. Collier and her daughters were also on the train. I'll give you their phone number so you can schedule an appointment."

Jonathon jotted down the number, then handed the slip of paper to Mr. Butler.

"Thank you. Good day, sir."

"Gentlemen." Jonathon glanced at Samuel standing in the back of the room. "Samuel, would you please show these men out?"

Samuel nodded, then led the men from the office. Jonathon blew out a breath, glad to hand the investigation over to them. In a way, he wished he could've given them his findings and his own solution. But he had plenty of other business to take care of. He strode to the window and crossed his arms, gazing at the lake. Several rowboats were scattered across on the other side, courtesy of the hotel, and other guests watched from the hotel's dock. He longed to be free to join them and enjoy the pleasant fall weather.

The image of Lettie Morgan's face entered his mind, and he could envision the two of them sharing a boat and skimming across the water. An idea struck him. Why not offer to take her out in a boat so she could take pictures from the lake instead of from the shore? Surely, she'd be agreeable to that idea. But when? Tonight, the Colliers were coming to dinner, and he had meetings the rest of the day. Tomorrow? Could he plan something so leisurely or be resigned to nothing but business?

What if she was out there now with one of the other gentlemen in town for the Assembly? His jaw twitched, and he grabbed the binoculars to see. Scanning the boats, he held his breath hoping he didn't see her in one. He scolded himself as he lowered the binoculars. Why should it bother him if she received another invitation? He had no entitlement to her time. He shook his head and looked away from the window. The stack of papers on his desk called him back, and he forced himself to return to work.

Chapter Six

Lettie inhaled the crisp fall air as she walked along the lakeshore toward the hotel, holding her camera securely by the leather strap on the top. After her experiment taking pictures of the ladies the day before, she decided to take more pictures of the guests. Then she could make a photo album with the pictures for the Assembly to keep. Would Jonathon Townsend like to have such a book? Whether he would or not, she was going to go forward with her idea. Even Aunt Gertie had encouraged her.

A few rowboats were on the lake, with happy couples sharing the joy of gliding through the calm water. She snapped a few pictures of them, then aimed at the dock and took photographs of people standing there. Those who weren't wearing hats carried lacy parasols, and when they noticed what she was doing, they began posing for her—some serious poses, some striking more humorous stances. She laughed along with them, enjoying every moment. After she had taken several pictures down by the water, she walked up the hill to the hotel to capture the guests there.

People sat on benches or stood in groups, while others relaxed on the large front veranda in rocking chairs or chaise lounges. Lettie didn't know if any of them were performers until she heard a woman laughing in the midst of a cluster of men and women. Lettie edged near, listening to the woman who had attracted the attention of the others. Her voice was loud, like she was familiar with projecting her voice from a stage. Her outrageous hat towered above the group, and as Lettie drew near, she stepped into an opening between a man and woman and snapped a picture.

The woman next to Lettie whispered in ear. "That's Helene Dupont, the actress."

Lettie's eyes widened. "*The* Helene Dupont?"

The other woman nodded. "Yes, isn't she amazing?"

Amazing wasn't the word Lettie had in mind, but certainly remarkable. Miss Dupont wasn't beautiful as one might expect, but she was striking. She moved with flourishes, as if dancing to a song no one else heard. Aware of the attention she garnered, she obviously devoured every bit of it. She smiled and laughed, swayed and turned, as if modeling her form-fitting dress with its revealing décolletage and showing off her hourglass figure. Her thick black hair had loosened from the upswept style under the hat, and escaped tendrils eased down her neck, one barely covering a dark birthmark just below her ear. Lettie had never seen a woman so bold but was delighted to observe her so closely. She wanted to take another photograph, but the woman wouldn't be still, and the picture would blur.

All of a sudden, Miss Dupont paused and looked straight at Lettie. She placed her hands on her hips and cocked her head. "And who's this pretty little thing? Are you the official photographer?"

Lettie's face heated. "Well, I'm, I guess you could say I am." A little fib couldn't hurt, could it? After all, no one else was taking pictures, not that she had seen anyway.

"Well, my dear, shoot away!" Miss Dupont affected a ludicrous pose, with one hand behind her head and the other on the hip she jutted out, then began moving through a series of bizarre poses. The crowd around her laughed, further embarrassing Lettie. Perhaps she'd overstepped her limits. "Well, why aren't you taking any pictures?" Miss Dupont asked.

"I … can't. Not while you're moving. You see, the photographs will be blurred."

"So, you're telling me to be still?" She grinned and winked, evoking more laughter from the crowd.

"That would be best for the picture." What else could she say? At least it was the truth.

"Well, in that case, I'll pretend I'm a statue, like the ones in Greece. I'll be the goddess Diana!" She affected another pose that drew more laughs, but this time Lettie took the photograph.

"Thank you," Lettie said.

"Surely, you'll want more than one! How about this?" Miss Dupont changed position again, and Lettie snapped another picture. Much as she wanted the actress's picture, she didn't want to use all her film on one subject, but she didn't know how to tell her, especially with all those people standing around.

That's when a gentleman walked up to Miss Dupont, with a broad smile and a distinctive English accent. "I see you're drawing a crowd again, Lovely." He lifted her hand and planted a lingering kiss on it. The actress beamed and swayed near him in a suggestive manner. Lettie took the opportunity to leave the circle, but as she turned away, a hand landed on her shoulder. She spun to see who it was, and Miss Dupont smiled at her.

"Come here, sweetie. I want you to meet my friend, Mr. Baxter Honeywell. Baxter, this is the official photographer of the Springlake Assembly. Isn't she adorable?"

Lettie's cheeks burned as the man took her hand and kissed the back of it. "It is indeed a pleasure to meet you. What is your name, dear?" His dark eyes penetrated her own in an unsettling fashion.

"Let, um, Loretta Morgan, sir."

He stood back and assessed her from top to bottom. "Ah, and you're a photographer. How charming."

Miss Dupont linked her arm through his elbow. "Baxter, why don't you let her take *our* photograph?" She gave him a knowing glance. "But you must be still and not cause the picture to blur. Isn't that right, Miss Morgan?"

Lettie nodded, her fingers sweating in her gloves as she held up the camera. The couple posed shoulder to shoulder, and Lettie snapped the photo, then Mr. Honeywell put his arm around the actress's waist and pulled her closer. Lettie snapped that photo as well but was embarrassed to witness such intimacy. She didn't know if they were courting or married, but one could certainly draw such a conclusion from their public display of affection.

Mr. Honeywell whispered something in Miss Dupont's ear, and she smiled.

"I believe we've monopolized your time long enough, Miss Morgan," Mr. Honeywell said dismissively. "Please excuse us."

Lettie nodded, but had no time to speak before the man took Miss Dupont's arm and led her away. But before they got out of earshot, the actress turned around toward Lettie and sent her a smile.

"You must come by tomorrow and join me for tea. I'd *love* to get to know you better."

The man at her side glanced back as well, but his lips formed a thin line, not the wide grin he'd had a few moments earlier.

As they walked away, the woman who had first spoken to Lettie appeared at her side. "You've been invited to tea with Miss Dupont! What an honor! Aren't you thrilled?"

"Yes, I am. And quite surprised as well. Do you think she meant it to be an invitation?"

"Absolutely! Oh, you *must* go! I wish she'd asked me."

Lettie glanced at the young woman, a sweet-faced girl dressed in very plain clothes, probably a student, and not one of means. "Is this your first time to come to the Springlake Assembly?"

"Yes, it is. I'm so excited to be here! My name is Mary, Mary Brown."

"It's nice to make your acquaintance, Mary. My name is Loretta Morgan, but please call me Lettie. Did you arrive on the train yesterday? The one that was robbed?"

The girl's face drained of what little color it had. "Oh dear Lord, yes. It was such a fright."

"And you saw the robber?"

"Yes. He was horrible! And so mean. I was so afraid he would kill us all."

"What did he look like?"

"Big. Big coat, big gun. Big voice. That's all I remember. I wanted to hide. I was afraid to look at him because he yelled at some of the passengers and said, "What are you staring at? Give me your valuables!""

"No wonder there's not much of a description. Seems like everyone says the same thing about him. And it sounds doubtful that anyone would recognize him if they saw him again."

Mary nodded. "We were all terrified. I hope I never see him again!"

"Well, I'm sure you won't. And now you can relax and enjoy your time here."

"Oh, I will. The trip was a Christmas gift from my grandmother. She knows how much I love to teach at our little schoolhouse. We live in a farming community, but there really aren't any schools for teachers where we live. Here at Springlake, I can learn about so many subjects that will make me a better teacher."

Lettie admired the woman's enthusiasm for her work and could understand her passion, since Lettie possessed the same kind of passion for her photography.

"What a nice gift. And you'll return with a gift of knowledge to share with your students."

Mary beamed. "I hope so." She looked at the camera in Lettie's hand. "And you're the Assembly's photographer?

What an honor."

Lettie smiled back but felt her face warming. "I wasn't actually asked to be the photographer, but it's my hobby. And since I'm here, I might as well take photos of everyone else, don't you think?"

"Of course, that makes sense. I wish I could see the photos when you finish."

An idea struck Lettie. "I think you shall. This roll of film is practically used up, and I'll have to mail the camera back to Kodak to be processed. But they're pretty prompt about returning it with a new roll, and I bet they can send back the processed photos within a couple of weeks."

"That would be wonderful. And then you'd show them to everyone?"

"Yes, I'll find a way to display them. I know Mr. Townsend, and I'm sure he'll approve."

Why did she say that when she hadn't even discussed it with him? Perhaps he wouldn't approve. What if he thought she was sticking her nose in his business? Or his guests'?

"You *know* him? I saw him yesterday afternoon when he came by the hotel and talked to Miss Dupont and Mr. Honeywell. He's a very handsome man!" Mary's eyes twinkled. "Just how well do you know him?"

Once again, Lettie's face heated and perspiration popped out along her hairline. "We're friends. My aunt knows his family." Although their friendship wasn't as close as her words suggested.

"You seem to know all the right people."

"Actually, I'm here with my aunt, Gertrude Ross. She's the one who knows everyone."

Mary's eyes widened and her mouth dropped open. "I'm very familiar with her work and I've read several of her books. I didn't even realize she would be here. I'd love to get her autograph."

"She'll be happy to give you one. She lives here just a couple of months in the fall until the Assembly is over. She has two other homes, one in California and one in New York, near where my parents live."

Mary's face was aglow with excitement. "Could you please introduce me to her while I'm here?"

"Of course. Let me check her schedule and I'll let you know when it's convenient."

Mary clasped her hands together. "What a wonderful Christmas this will be, being here and getting to meet such a prestigious author." She placed her hand on Lettie's free one and squeezed it. "I'm so happy we met, Lettie!"

Lettie smiled back, pleased that she'd made Mary so happy. Her small gesture was like a special gift to Mary, a Christmas gift. Lettie had barely even thought about Christmas, perhaps because it didn't feel like Christmas here in Springlake, certainly not like any Christmas she'd ever had. Christmas in New York meant cold and snow, lots of snow. Here in this balmy environment of the Florida panhandle, the air was just barely cool, more like a May day in upstate New York. Not only didn't it feel like Christmas, it didn't look like Christmas either. Where were the Christmas trees? The decorations? She hadn't seen any since she'd arrived.

Of course, it was still November, so the Christmas decorations probably wouldn't go up until December. But how much did they decorate down here in the south? They couldn't add snow, and the lake would never freeze over so they could ice-skate. Would Aunt Gertie know? Perhaps she should ask Mr. Townsend about it. She needed to ask him about the photographs anyway. A ripple of energy coursed through her with the prospect of speaking with him. But she pushed it down. Her purpose was purely professional, and nothing else. Besides, his affections were set on Caroline Collier anyway.

Lettie took a few more pictures, almost reaching the limit of one hundred on the roll. The sooner she mailed the camera in, the sooner she'd get it back, as well as the photographs. As she glanced toward the lake, she saw a flock of geese soaring in, skidding to a landing with a splash right behind Mr. Townsend's house. She might as well finish off the roll with more photographs of the interesting waterfowl, so she took the path around the lake. At the end of the fence, she noticed a bench placed beside the water. She glanced up the hill toward the house. Did Mr. Townsend place the bench there because of her suggestion? Well, he did tell her she was welcome to take photos from his property, so she proceeded to the bench, a little bubble of delight that he'd accepted her idea. What a nice thing for him to do.

She positioned herself on the bench and used up the rest of her film, delighted and entertained by the birds' antics. When one large goose headed her way squawking a warning, she jumped up and backed away, but the goose continued advancing.

"Shoo! Go away!" She waved her hand at him.

Voices from the Townsend Mansion sounded behind her, and she glanced over her shoulder to see who was there. Several women stood on the large veranda overlooking the lake, their laughter reaching her ears. One of them was Caroline Collier, two were older women and one was a girl in her teens. Only one man stood with them—Jonathon Townsend. Lettie's face burned at the thought that she might be the object of their laughter. She turned toward the public path and hurried away, hoping to find a way out of their sight.

Chapter Seven

Jonathon watched Lettie Morgan scurry away. He'd been delighted to see she'd availed herself of the bench he'd had moved to the water's edge. If only Caroline and her family hadn't been with him. He would have gone down to greet her and find out if she appreciated his gesture. But unfortunately, they'd all walked out on the veranda just as the geese were acting up, one in particular appeared to be stalking Miss Morgan. She'd handled herself well, despite the goose's threat, but his company found the whole episode humorous. A thought gripped him. Did Miss Morgan think they were laughing at her? He certainly hoped not.

He owed her an apology, not that he'd done anything wrong, but he didn't want her thinking the worst. His gaze followed her until she was out of sight, wishing he could go after her and straighten things out. Someone clasped his elbow and he glanced down to see Caroline's gloved hands around his arm.

"Jonathon! Cat got your tongue?" Caroline peered up at him, eyes sparkling.

"I'm sorry. I didn't hear what you were saying."

"We were talking about the performers who will be at the Assembly this year, in particular, Miss Dupont. Have you met her?"

"Yes, I did. I needed to speak with her about the train

robbery."

"And what did you think of her?" Caroline eyed him curiously.

"Think of her? We only spoke a brief time, so I haven't seen her perform."

"I think she's sassy!" Constance blurted out, with her hands on her hips.

"Constance!" Her mother said. "Mind your manners."

"Well she is!" Constance stuck out her lips. "Don't you think so, Mr. Jonathon?"

His collar tightened. "I think I'd describe her as high-spirited, yes, that's it."

"She's attractive, don't you agree?" Caroline asked, her expression daring him to say "yes."

"I suppose so, in her own way, but not lovely like you ladies." Jonathon hoped his answer would satisfy her curiosity. Her blush confirmed his intention.

"I hear she's quite a singer and has a repertoire of everything from Vaudeville to opera," Mrs. Collier said.

"How interesting," Mother said. "I can't imagine singing the two extremes." Mother rubbed her arms. "It's getting cool out here. Shall we go inside? I believe dinner is almost ready."

The group went inside, but Jonathon lingered back, hoping to catch another glimpse of Miss Morgan.

"Come on, Jonathon," Caroline grabbed his hand and pulled him into the house. "They're just geese."

Jonathon found Caroline's perspective such a contrast to Lettie, who considered the birds to be works of art themselves. She appreciated nature and the fascinating variety the Creator had made, and thanks to her, he was beginning to appreciate it too.

The conversation at dinner revolved around the Collier's grand three-month tour to Europe, where they landed in Ireland and traveled through several countries, ending in Italy. They had traveled onboard the RMS Baltic of the

White Start Line, one of the largest ships of the fleet, and certainly one of the grandest. Much of the conversation revolved around who else was onboard and what they wore. Bored with the social talk, Jonathon focused on the intricate design of the William Morris wallpaper with magnolia blossoms among rich green leaves. Grandmother had insisted on having Morris wallpaper in every room when she decorated the interior of the house. And of course, she had to have magnolias somewhere in every room, even carved into the mahogany staircase.

He vaguely heard Mother suggest they retire to the parlor and followed the rest of the group instinctively, as if he were an automaton, stepping back to enter the parlor when Samuel slid open the large wooden pocket doors, allowing the women to enter first. His ears perked up when Caroline's mother spoke of their visit to Pompeii, the topic stirring Jonathon's jealousy, for he had not had time to visit that part of the world when his trip to Europe had been cut short by Father's sudden illness, and Jonathon wondered if he'd ever return. The Colliers had brought their vast collection of postcards to show him and his mother.

"We're going to make albums with them!" Caroline's little sister pointed to a stack of postcards. "All of these came from France, so they'll go into a France album. Those over there will be in a Switzerland album, and those will be in an England album."

Jonathon eyed a postcard with a lighthouse on it, pushing down another twinge of envy for not being able to see the site in person himself. He half-listened to the conversation while his mind wandered to the image of Miss Morgan's hasty retreat from the property. He winced at the insult she may have felt, and he needed to find her and express his regret for the episode. Each loud tick from the grandfather clock in the foyer pricked his heart with remorse as the clock conspired to slow down time. Good thing he couldn't see the clock from where he sat or he'd be staring at it, willing it to move so the evening would end, and Caroline and her family would leave.

"Did the Pinkertons come by your house today?" Jonathon's question halted conversation and all eyes focused on him.

"Yes, they did."

Mother sent him a scornful glance. "Must we discuss that now, Jonathon?"

Caroline offered a sympathetic smile. "I don't mind, Mrs. Townsend. I know it's important to Jonathon, to all of us actually, to find out who the robber was and what happened to him."

Ignoring his mother's rebuke, Jonathon pursued the topic. "Yes, it is important, and the sooner we know, the better."

"I'm afraid we couldn't give them any additional information, though," Caroline said.

"I don't suppose they mentioned any findings to you?" Not that he thought they would.

"No, not at all. They were pretty tight-lipped."

"I told them I'd find answers for them!" Constance asserted. "I could be quite a sleuth."

"Constance, do be serious," Mrs. Collier chided. "I'm certain they don't need your help."

Constance pursed her lips as her mother and sister frowned at her.

Mrs. Collier glanced around, then stood. "I'm afraid it's time for us to leave. I've been tiring easily, and I believe I'm still adjusting to being back home on solid land. Sometimes I feel as though I'm still on the ship." She faced Mother. "Thank you so much for your hospitality." She nodded a slight bow, and Mother smiled and nodded in return. Her daughters stood as well, and Caroline extended her hand to Jonathon.

"Thank you so much, Jonathon. I enjoyed discussing the sights in Europe with you."

Jonathon took her hand and clasped it between his. "And I did with you as well." He noted a look of disappointment in her eyes. No doubt she expected him to kiss her hand. But he didn't want her to assume his feelings were any more than they were. Lettie Morgan's face flashed through his mind with a certainty that he would have no hesitation if it were her hand that was offered. But her lips held an even greater attraction. His collar tightened as he bid their guests goodbye and hoped they couldn't read his mind.

Lettie avoided going anywhere near Jonathon's house after the humiliation she endured. Although she needed to pass his house when walking a fairly short distance, if she were in the car, she'd go around the lake the opposite way. In fact, she did indeed drive the car to the hotel the next afternoon when she met Helene Dupont for tea.

Miss Dupont insisted they have tea outside her room on the balcony instead of in the dining room so they could have more privacy. Miss Dupont's sheer lounging gown and kimono weren't typical of the way most women dressed for tea. But then Miss Dupont was anything but typical. And even though she'd sought privacy, her hearty laugh drew attention to them anyway, so other guests looked up and waved, and the actress waved in return. Lettie questioned whether her motive to be on the balcony was more attention-getting than private. The Shakespeare quote, "All the world's a stage," came to Lettie's mind.

Their conversation mostly revolved around the adventures of Miss Dupont, and Lettie was fascinated by all the places the woman had performed.

"You really rode an elephant?"

The actress laughed and gave a firm nod of her head. "I certainly did! Gave that elephant the ride of his life!"

Lettie couldn't hold back her own laughter at the actress's turn of the phrase. "You have such an exciting life. Someday, I'd like to travel the world and take photos of everything and everybody I see."

The actress's face grew solemn, and she leaned forward toward Lettie. "And you will. You have your whole life ahead of you. Just promise me you'll stay true to yourself, and don't let any man steal your dream."

Lettie wanted to ask what she meant, and if that had happened to her, but she didn't want to pry into the woman's personal affairs. Was the actress warning her to protect her virtue? Why would she say that? Did she not think Lettie's morals were strong?

"Well, you've succeeded in reaching your dreams."

Miss Dupont's smile returned. "I certainly have."

"And I will, too. Perhaps I can convince my aunt to go along as my chaperone."

"Now that's an idea!"

Lettie frowned. "Aunt Gertie says she's finished with traveling, though. She says she's seen all she wants to see now and is happy with where she is—which is any one of her three homes, New York, Springlake, or California."

"So, when do I get to see those photographs you took of me?"

"As soon as I can get them back from processing. Which reminds me that my next stop is the post office, so I can mail the camera to Kodak."

Miss Dupont waved her away. "I've enjoyed our tea, but I don't want to keep you from your business. You can come back and visit another time. In fact, I insist that you do."

Business? Ah, yes, she'd told everyone she was the Assembly photographer. The only problem was she hadn't told the people in charge of the Assembly yet, and the only person she knew in that role was Jonathon Townsend. And she had no idea when she'd see him again. Lettie stood and brushed off her skirt. "I've really enjoyed our conversation."

"Same here. Do you mind finding your way out? I'm rather tired."

"Oh, I don't mind at all. You stay right there and rest." Lettie went back inside and walked through the actress's room toward the door. She couldn't help but notice the variety of clothing hanging around the room, some draped over a dressing screen, some draped over the sofa. She tried not to ogle too much before she reached the door. She opened it as Baxter Honeywell stood with his hand poised to knock.

His brow creased and his eyes widened in surprise when he saw her, but a slow smile crept across his face. He tipped his hat. "Good afternoon, Miss …"

"It's Morgan. Loretta Morgan. I was just having tea with Miss Dupont."

"Ah, yes, she did mention that. Did you two ladies enjoy yourselves?"

"Yes, we did. I look forward to the next time."

His eyebrows arched. "You two are making this a routine?"

"I suppose that's up to Miss Dupont." Lettie edged past him into the hallway. "Please excuse me, I need to run an errand."

He gave a slight bow. "Please do not let me get in your way. Good day, Miss Morgan."

"Good day, Mr. Honeywell." She hurried away, sensing she was keeping him from Miss Dupont. Were they more than good friends? It wasn't her business, but there was something about that man Lettie didn't like—his shifty black eyes or the insincere smiles he gave. Perhaps she was judging the man unfairly, but she was uncomfortable around him. Plus he also acted as if she was intruding on him and Miss Dupont, or so it seemed.

Since she'd driven the car, Lettie was thankful when one of the men in front of the hotel offered to turn the crank for her. Driving a car was easy, in her opinion, but sometimes the crank was hard to turn, a feature many people believed was the reason only men should drive. Maybe she should write to Mr. Ford and ask him to make starting cars easier. She could just imagine the laugh such a letter would receive.

Lettie drove to the mercantile and left the car running when she ran into the store. The post office was in the back corner of the store, and she set her camera on the counter.

"Would you please mail this back to the Kodak company for me?"

The clerk eyed her. "Used up 100 pictures already?"

"Yes, sir, I sure did. I've taken pictures of the entire lake area and many of the Assembly guests. Unfortunately, I've run out of film. Do you know how long it will take to get the film processed?"

The man shrugged. "Can't say. I've only mailed a couple of these Brownies back before, and I can't remember how long it was before the pictures came back. Two, maybe three weeks, I'm guessing."

Lettie's heart sank. "That long? Oh dear."

"They usually send the camera back with new film before the pictures come back."

"But how long does that take?"

"Ma'am, I wish I could help you, but I don't know how to make the mail or the Kodak company move any faster."

"Of course you can't. I just wish I'd turned it in sooner. I'd like to get the photographs back before the Assembly is over."

"We'll hope for the best." The man took the camera and wrapped it in parchment paper, then tied it with string. He wrote the Kodak address on it, with Aunt Gertie's return address. "That'll be twenty-five cents," he said, holding out his hand. Lettie paid him the money, then thanked him and turned to go.

She stopped on her way out to look at the new cameras in the store.

"Miss Morgan?"

Lettie jerked at the sound of Jonathon Townsend's voice beside her. She glanced around to see if anyone else was with him and also to see how she could avoid him. But she was trapped in the aisle. Her face heated, but she sucked in a breath for composure.

"Hello, Mr. Townsend," she said as coolly as possible.

"Are you thinking about buying another camera? Has yours quit working?"

The sincerity in his eyes threatened to unnerve her. How could he sound so caring when she knew his true affection was toward Caroline Collier?

"No. Mine works fine. I just had to send it back to Kodak to process the film, since I used all one hundred images."

"You've taken that many pictures? You've been very busy."

She glanced away, remembering how his guests had laughed at her by the lake.

He cleared his throat. "Miss Morgan, I owe you an apology. Last night when we were outside on our veranda, the women got a little too amused at the antics of the geese. When I saw you rush away, I feared you thought they were laughing at you."

She cut her eyes at him. "And they weren't?"

"No, absolutely not. They didn't even mention you. They only talked about the geese. I'm sorry if you thought otherwise."

She expelled a breath. "I did. That nosy gander wouldn't leave me alone."

Mr. Townsend smiled. "He's a male, and you know we males can sometimes act pretty unruly."

She smiled in return. How could she stay angry with such a gentleman?

His face sobered and his gaze focused on her. "Actually, I had hoped you would be able to enjoy sitting on the bench while you took your photographs."

"You put the bench there for me?" Her pulse quickened.

He nodded. "I did. You had suggested we have a stationary place from which to enjoy the lake, so I took your suggestion to heart and had the bench placed there."

"That was very thoughtful of you. Apparently, the goose didn't appreciate the gesture, though. Or my presence."

"Perhaps I need to teach that goose a lesson in hospitality. Maybe we should have goose on the menu for Christmas dinner." He gave a slight wink.

"You wouldn't! Oh, please don't harm him. I'll just try to stay out of his way."

He laughed at her reaction as she steeled herself to tell him about her little lie.

"I'm afraid I have a confession to make to you," Lettie said.

He drew back. "Oh dear. What horrible thing have you done?" His eyes twinkled with amusement.

"I've used up all my film because I've been taking pictures of the guests at the hotel and by the lake, and elsewhere. When they asked me if I was the official Assembly photographer, I said I was."

He crossed his arms, his fingertip on his chin. "Is that right? Actually, that's not a bad idea. Since we don't have another photographer, I pronounce you the official Assembly photographer."

Lettie's face broke into a grin. "Do you mean that, or are you just teasing me?"

He took her hand, sending a jolt up her arm. "I assure you, I am quite sincere."

Excitement mingled with anxiety. "I thought it would be nice to post the pictures on the wall or in an album, so the guests could enjoy them."

"That's a wonderful idea! More and more of our presenters are arriving each day, and it would be a nice memento to have for future Assembly attendees to see."

Her enthusiasm dimmed, and she looked away. "I'm not

sure the photographs will be back in time though. Plus, I can't take anymore photos until Kodak returns the reloaded camera. I don't know how long that will take."

"Hmm. That could be a problem. Tell you what. Let me buy you another camera to use in the meantime."

"No, you can't do that."

"Of course I can. I'm director of the Assembly and you're the Assembly photographer, so I need to make sure you have the equipment you need to do your job." He opened the glass case and took out a new camera, then handed it to her.

She took it as if it might break in her hands, her mouth agape. How could she refuse?

"Thank you. But I don't know if the photographs will be returned in time for this year's attendees to see."

"You let me handle that. My grandfather was friends with Mr. Eastman, and he knew my father as well. Perhaps a little conversation with him can expedite your film being processed."

"I don't know what to say. I can't believe you would do this for me."

His eyes softened, and they penetrated hers. "I am happy to do whatever I can for you. I want you to think of me as a friend, a very good friend, if nothing else. Can you do that?"

She nodded, words escaping her. What did he mean by that?

"But I would like to ask you a favor."

Her back stiffened. So, there was a catch. "What?"

"Will you please call me Jonathon? And may I please call you Loretta?"

She shook her head. "No."

He looked shocked and even hurt. "Why not?"

"I can call you Jonathon. But please don't call me Loretta. Call me Lettie."

Chapter Eight

Every day, more people arrived for the Assembly, filling up the Springlake Hotel as well as the other downtown hotel.

Other people like Gertrude Ross who owned cottages on the lake but only occupied them during the season also came into town and opened their winter homes. Some of them even hosted some of the special guests. Reverend Leland Anderson stayed with the Fraziers, and Reverend John Peterson stayed with the Mr. and Mrs. Henderson. Of course, Mother insisted Dr. James Butler stay with them. Dr. Butler and his wife had been friends of her and Father for many years.

Jonathon was thankful every time the train arrived in town without another robbery. He would have been appalled had any of the ministers been robbed, especially Dr. Butler. The thief had not been caught yet, and the Pinkertons seemed no closer to solving the mystery. They had not ruled out the possibility that the man had exited the train along with everyone else, undetected, and was then picked up by his partner. But so far, no one had been captured.

He hadn't spoken to Lettie Morgan much since he bought her the camera, and only spotted her occasionally along the shore taking pictures. Whenever he caught her attention, she waved, and he waved back. If only he could spend more time with her. But he'd been so busy, he hadn't had the opportunity. He was in his office when the chime sounded from the front door. He glanced at his pocket watch. Did he have an appointment?

Samuel's voice came over the intercom. "Mr. Townsend, there's someone here to see you."

Jonathon pushed the button on the wall to speak. "May I ask who he is?"

"He is a she. Her name is Miss Lettie Morgan."

Jonathon jumped up grabbed his jacket. "Tell her I'll be right down."

"Yes, sir."

He shrugged into his jacket as he trotted down the stairs. Why had she come?

Lettie stood just inside the stained-glass double doors, her eyes scanning the room. His heart beat even faster at the sight of her. She was radiant, her honey-blond hair framing her face beneath a straw hat with its black ribbon hanging down the back. She wore a green traveling suit that accentuated her perfectly proportioned shape. When she saw him, she flashed a smile that melted his insides.

"Lettie!" He reached out to take her hands in his. "How nice to see you! Please come in."

Lettie glanced around. "I'm sorry to interrupt you like this."

"I welcome the interruption. Please, come on in." He gestured to the solarium where she entered and took a seat. "Is anything wrong?"

"No, well, maybe."

"What can I do? Is there a problem with your camera? You received the first photos, didn't you?"

"The camera's fine, and yes, I got the photographs. That's not what I want to discuss with you. You know, the Assembly starts the first day of December, in just a few days. But December is Christmastime, and there aren't any Christmas decorations around here! Of course, it won't snow here, but there are no other reminders that Christmas is approaching."

Jonathon stroked his chin. "You're right, we don't have any decorations. But closer to Christmas, we'll have a nativity set up in the church."

"That's good, and there definitely should be, but what about the rest of the area? The Assembly Hall is a very plain, white structure, other than the columns on the front. What about putting up some wreaths?"

"We can do that."

"And a Christmas tree? The lobby of the hall is tall enough for a nice big tree."

"Hmm. Yes, it is. I can ask one of the local farmers if they have a tree we can use. But what about ornaments? It will take a lot."

"We can host an ornament-making party and let those who are interested come and contribute their creations to the tree."

"Another good idea. I can tell you've thought about this quite a bit."

"I have, and I think it would add to the experience for the attendees."

"No doubt it would. Will you help with the decorations?"

"Of course! But do you know anyone else who can help?"

The front door opened, and the sound of Mother's voice entered the house, along with Dr. Butler's. Jonathon also heard Samuel speaking in a low tone, apparently telling Mother and the minister that he and Lettie were present. A moment later, the two of them entered the solarium.

Jonathon and Lettie stood. "Mother. Dr. Butler. I'd like you to meet a friend of mine, Lettie Morgan. She's Gertrude Ross's niece."

Mother eyed Lettie, then glanced at Jonathon with a knowing look.

Lettie dipped a slight curtsy. "Nice to meet you, Mrs. Townsend, Dr. Butler."

"It's very nice to meet you, too, dear. I've heard that you're responsible for taking all the photographs," Mrs. Townsend said.

Lettie blushed. "Yes, ma'am, I am."

Dr. Butler bowed, then excused himself to his room.

"Mother, Lettie has some ideas that perhaps you could help her with."

Mother's eyebrows lifted. "That so? What kind of ideas do you have, dear?"

Lettie recapped the suggestions she'd given to Jonathon. "Do you know anyone who might like to help?"

Mother's eyes widened. "Well, yes I do! My lady's club would love to help."

"Could they manage the decoration-making party? We could hold it in one of the rooms in the Assembly Hall, but we should do so this weekend or next, so the decorations will be ready when we get the tree."

Mother clapped her hands. "What a marvelous idea! I'll get started making a flyer as soon as I speak to my club members and decide when to have the party."

Jonathon watched the interaction between Lettie and his mother, elated to see the women getting along so well. Mother really appeared to like Lettie. *Thank God*, he breathed.

Funny that he hadn't even thought about Christmas approaching. With all the details of the Assembly to handle, as well as, the other businesses, Christmas had been pushed to the rear of his mind. The idea of decorating Springlake had already put him in a festive mood. But Christmas also meant gifts, and he hadn't given any thought to those either. Not that he had many people to buy gifts for. Normally, he only bought gifts for his mother and father. And Samuel usually got a bonus. This year, it was just Mother and Samuel. And Lettie. He wanted to give her a gift too, but what?

A pall of sadness fell over him. Christmas also meant Lettie would be leaving soon, going to California with her aunt. And he wasn't certain she'd ever be returning to Springlake. She had shared her desire to travel the world when they first met, and he was certain she'd find a way to accomplish her desire. As he watched Mother and Lettie excitedly discuss their plans, Jonathon knew he wanted Lettie to stay. But how could he convince her, especially with her aunt leaving and closing up her cottage? She certainly wouldn't leave her niece alone in the house. What could he do?

Lettie really liked Mrs. Townsend. She was quite friendly and easy to carry on a conversation with. The woman had dark hair with silver streaks running through it, just enough to add an air of sophistication. She wore a high-necked white lace blouse with a sapphire broach at the neckline under her royal blue jacket and matching skirt. She carried herself like a queen, albeit a friendly queen. Her eyes twinkled with excitement as she and Lettie exchanged ideas.

A hint of sadness tugged at her heart when she realized Mrs. Townsend would be Caroline Collier's mother-in-law someday. Lucky girl. Lettie hoped that when she married, she'd have a mother-in-law as pleasant.

Lettie let her gaze roam around the lovely, sunlit solarium. A number of parlor palms and ferns lined the windowed round walls, while inviting wicker chairs and chaise lounges provided comfort. A glance at the floor made Lettie smile. The pattern inlaid in the wood floor was the Flying Geese pattern. How appropriate, since there were many geese right behind the house. Was this pattern intentional?

Small, stained-glass windows adorned the tops of the tall windows lining the round room. A magnolia blossom occupied the center of each window, mirroring the magnolias in the stained glass of the front door. No wonder this was called the Magnolia Manor. And she'd thought it was due to the magnolia trees on either side of the house.

"I heard your photographs line the entry wall of the Assembly Hall. I hope to see them soon," Mrs. Townsend said.

"Oh, please do! I'm asking each person who sees himself or herself in the photo write their name and the date at the bottom. That way, we'll still know who they are once the pictures are put in the Assembly photo album so future attendees can see them."

"What a splendid idea!"

"Speaking of ideas, ladies, might I offer one?" Jonathon said.

He'd been silent while the women talked, and Lettie almost forgot he was still in the room. Both women turned to face him.

"Yes, Jonathon. What do you suggest?" his mother asked.

"While you ladies were talking about a party, I thought about a different kind of party. Not that I'm opposed to the ladies meeting to create decorations, but what about having a real party, such as a ball, a formal Christmas ball?"

Lettie and Mrs. Townsend exchanged glances.

Jonathon continued. "I was thinking that, in light of the inconvenience some of the attendees experienced with the robbery, we should do something special to give them fond memories of the Assembly."

"Why, Jonathon, that's an excellent idea. What do you think, Lettie?"

"I agree it's a grand idea as well. However, what if the Assembly attendees don't have formal clothes to wear?" She wasn't sure what she would wear to such an occasion, either, but she might have something that would do. However, she was certain people like Mary Brown wouldn't have any dresses appropriate for formal balls. "They might feel excluded."

"That's a good point," Jonathon said. "I know some of our attendees are students of limited means."

"Then we must promote it as a Christmas party open to all, formal attire optional," Mrs. Townsend said.

"So you'd like to proceed with plans for it?" Jonathon asked.

"Absolutely!" Mrs. Townsend clasped her hands. "Well, I must get busy. I have quite a lot to do, if you'd like me to organize the affair."

"I hope you don't mind, Mother. I don't mean to put undue stress on you."

Mrs. Townsend waved him away. "Jonathon, I've organized events such as this all my life. I just haven't had as much to do since your father passed away." She looked down at her lap as if gathering herself, then glanced up with a smile. "I'm looking forward to being involved in something pleasurable. In fact, I'm very excited and eager to get started." She looked over at Lettie. "Besides, I won't be handling all the work myself. I'm sure Miss Morgan will help, won't you dear?"

"Oh yes! I'd love to. Just let me know what you'd like me to do. I can take photographs at the ball of course."

"You may take photographs if you wish, but I want you to enjoy the ball too. I'm sure there are some young gentlemen who would like to have your dance card." Mrs. Townsend sent Jonathon a knowing glance.

Jonathon's face reddened under his mother's gaze, but he nodded and smiled as he looked at Lettie. "I just hope you leave room for me on your card, Lettie."

Chapter Nine

"A Christmas ball! How exciting!" Aunt Gertie's face brightened. "I don't think we've ever had one of those here. It will be a fitting and happy conclusion to the Assembly. Aren't you excited?" She sat on the settee and patted the ottoman for Lettie to come sit too.

Lettie shrugged, then sank onto the ottoman. "I suppose so, but I really don't know what to think about it."

"What's to think about? It's a party, a dance!" Aunt Gertie waved her hands in the air for emphasis. "Why, if I were a young, unmarried girl like you, I'd be over the moon with excitement. So why aren't you?"

"First of all, I don't know what to wear. I didn't bring any Christmas gowns. And besides that, even though Jonathon said he wanted to dance with me, I don't know if he's planning to be my escort or just see me there."

"I can't answer your question about Jonathon. But I can help you with the gown."

"You can? How?"

Aunt Gertie stood and crooked her finger at Lettie. "Come with me."

Lettie followed her aunt into her bedroom where the woman walked over to a trunk at the foot of the bed and opened it. Reaching inside, Aunt Gertie's fingers gently dug through layers until she found a tissue-wrapped bundle. She pulled it out and handed it to Lettie.

"What is this?"

"Open it."

Lettie slid her fingers along the folds of the paper and carefully pulled open the wrapping. When she saw the contents, she sucked in a breath. "What is this?"

"Go ahead. Hold it up."

Lettie lifted the ruby red taffeta dress with black lace overlay on the bodice and sleeves, letting the dress unfold until it was fully extended. She gasped. "Aunt Gertie, this is gorgeous."

"I thought so too."

Lettie ran her finger over the black rose with a long stem that was embroidered onto the front of the dress, matching the black lace on the top and bottom of the dress.

"Whose is it? Where did you get it?"

"I bought it in Paris the last time I was there, three years ago. When I saw the dress, I knew it would be lovely on you, but I didn't think you were old enough to wear it then. I saved it until you would be, planning to give it to you for a special occasion. Now is the perfect time for you to have it."

Her eyes filled with tears, Lettie held the dress against her and glanced at her reflection in the cheval mirror. "I can't believe you bought this for me. It's exquisite."

"Try it on. I can't wait to see it on you."

Lettie slipped out of her skirt and removed her blouse, then she stepped into the dress and pulled it up. The dress flowed to the floor, covering the tips of Lettie's shoes. Aunt Gertie buttoned the covered buttons that ran down the back of the dress while Lettie stood in front of the mirror. Aunt Gertie stepped from behind her and admired the dress on Lettie.

"It's a perfect fit, just as I thought it would be." Aunt Gertie beamed, her eyes bright with unshed tears. "All the young men will trip over themselves to get a dance with you."

Who was the woman in the mirror? Lettie couldn't believe she was looking at her own reflection. That person evoked dignity and poise, so unlike herself. And yet, it was Lettie Morgan, rather Loretta Morgan, who returned her gaze. She pulled her shoulders back, straightened her spine and lifted her chin, noticing how mature the reflection appeared.

Aunt Gertie walked to her dresser, opened a drawer and retrieved a pair of elbow-length black gloves, then handed them to Lettie. Next, she opened an accessory drawer and withdrew a black hair comb adorned with what appeared to be rubies, offering it to Lettie. "This will be perfect in your hair." She held it up against Lettie's hair. "Oh! And I have the finishing touch." She opened another drawer and held up a black ostrich feather. "What do you think?"

Lettie's aunt positioned the feather so that it appeared to come out of Lettie's hair. "I don't know about the feather, Aunt Gertie. Perhaps just the comb. Or if I had an elegant headband..."

"We'll check the stores in town. If they don't have any, maybe we could order it from the Sears Roebuck catalog."

"It's not that important. With such a perfect dress, no one will notice my hair anyway."

"Good thing you have such lovely hair."

"Thank you so much, Aunt Gertie. I still can't believe you bought this for me."

"You are quite welcome. I wish your parents could see you. Now, let's get you out of it. It needs to hang and air out so it will be fresh and unwrinkled by the ball." Aunt Gertie unbuttoned the dress, and Lettie stepped out of it. As her aunt hung the dress on a hanger, she spoke over her shoulder to Lettie. "Trust me, Lettie, Jonathon Townsend will be mesmerized when he sees you in this dress."

Would he? What if Caroline Collier gained his attention instead?

Soon, the Assembly Hall was festooned in Christmas decorations. Wreaths adorned each door, garlands draped the doorways, and a huge tree stood in the main entry, loaded with an assortment of handmade ornaments. The women in town had joined the women attending the Assembly to create festive decorations that were placed all over Springlake, including the train depot. A festive spirit permeated the atmosphere, and smiles were in abundance.

Lettie tried to attend every lecture and performance, soaking in the inspirational speakers and enjoying the entertainment from the musicians and performers. Aunt Gertie accompanied Lettie to most of the events, but when her aunt didn't come, Lettie sought out Mary Brown for company. She seldom saw Jonathon except at a distance, as he seemed preoccupied with managing affairs of the event.

Lettie and Mary agreed to meet for the next performance by Helene Dupont. She'd had tea with her once more before the opening day of the Assembly, but after that, they were both too busy to meet. Miss Dupont swept onstage with a flourish dressed in an oriental costume and sang an operatic song. The audience erupted with applause, then Miss Dupont left the stage while a storyteller came on and told a humorous tale. When he was finished, Miss Dupont returned to the stage, this time as a cowgirl and sang some rather rowdy western ballads.

"She has quite a vocal range, doesn't she?" Mary whispered in Lettie's ear.

"I was just thinking the same thing. She can hit the high notes of the opera as well as the low notes in the ballads. She is quite talented."

Miss Dupont left the stage again, and the storyteller returned to share another tale.

The next time the actress appeared, she was dressed as a French can-can girl, kicking up her heels to dance as the orchestra played. Her statuesque presence filled the stage, and when she finished her performance, she bowed low to accept the enthusiastic applause of the audience.

"Are you going to the ball?" Lettie whispered to her friend while waiting for the next act.

Mary glanced down and shook her head. "I'd like to, but I just don't have anything to wear but the same old suit and blouse I've worn every day."

Lettie placed her hand on Mary's arm. "But you must come. The flyer says you only need to dress up if you care to."

"But I care to, and I can't."

"We're about the same size, aren't we? I bet I have something you can wear."

"But I couldn't."

"Nonsense. Come with me afterwards."

"All right, if you insist."

All of a sudden, Jonathon slid into the seat on the other side of Lettie. Her heart raced, and her face grew hot.

"I've been looking for you."

"You have?" She'd looked for him as well but wouldn't admit it.

Another lecture had started, and heads turned to look at them, showing annoyance at their talking during the presentation.

"Yes, meet me outside so we can talk when this is over."

"All right."

He squeezed her hand, then left.

Mary glanced sideways at Lettie and smiled.

Lettie tried to appear nonchalant and shrugged, but inside her heart was running away with itself. The minutes dragged by as the speaker continued, and Lettie had no idea what he said. She just wanted him to stop so she could leave. But she didn't want to leave too soon and appear too eager to speak with Jonathon.

Finally, the lecture ended. Mary and Lettie stood. "I need to meet him outside, but I want you to wait for me so we can go to my aunt's house together."

"All right. I'll look at the photos in the foyer until you're finished with your conversation. But if you need to leave with him, I'll understand."

"I'm not going anywhere with him right now, so don't worry about it."

Lettie found Jonathon standing in the foyer studying the photos with a number of other people. She tapped him on the shoulder, and he turned around, his frown turning into a broad smile.

"There you are." He took her elbow and led her outside away from the crowd.

"So you've been looking for me?" Lettie cocked her head to look up at him in the afternoon sunlight.

He took her hands in his. "Yes, ma'am. I wanted to ask if you'll allow me to escort you to the ball."

Lettie's mouth opened, but she couldn't find the words to speak. What about Caroline Collier, she wanted to ask. But that wouldn't be appropriate. She searched his face as he peered intently into hers, waiting for an answer. She swallowed, hoping to remedy the dryness in her mouth.

A slow smile eased across his face emitting warmth that melted her resolve.

"I'd like that," she said, her words barely above a whisper.

He leaned closer to her, gently squeezing her hands as he lifted them to his lips and kissed them. "I was hoping you'd accept."

They stared at each other in silence while her heart thumped against her ribcage. They might have stayed that way forever if a gentleman hadn't approached, clearing his throat.

"Please pardon the interruption, Mr. Townsend. You're

wanted in the exhibit hall."

The spell broken, Jonathon released her hands and sighed. "Business calls, I'm afraid." A frown had returned to his handsome face.

"Is anything wrong?"

"Hopefully not. The Pinkertons suggested that the robber could be one of the attendees that managed to disembark here in Springlake unnoticed."

"But how could that have happened? He was seen jumping from the train."

"The Pinkertons doubt that, since they've found no trace of him. And if he didn't leave the train sooner, he could have stayed on it until it reached here."

"But what about those who said he jumped off?"

"The detectives think those people imagined or created that scenario, when it could've just been conjecture."

"So he could be here? Among us? But where would he have hidden on the train?"

Jonathon nodded. "Perhaps the baggage car. But don't worry, we're going to have extra guards for the ball, just in case."

Lettie's eyes widened. "The ball? Do you truly believe the robber could be so bold as to appear at the ball?"

"Actually, I don't. On the other hand, the robber could take advantage of the ball to rob the hotel rooms of the guests, so we're going to station guards there also." He gave her a sincere smile. "You don't need to be concerned, Lettie. I won't let anyone harm you. I pray the scoundrel will be caught before he can do any more harm. Besides, I don't want anything to spoil our evening together." He took a few steps away, then paused and looked back.

"Oh, I meant to tell you … don't go behind my house for the time being. We've had quite a few snakes reported back there, so we don't want anyone going near the area until we can get rid of them."

"Snakes?" She placed her hand over her heart. "My

goodness. I'll certainly stay clear of the area."

As he walked away, Lettie blew out a breath and tried to calm herself. She glanced around at the people milling about, realizing she'd not noticed anyone else when she and Jonathon were together, as if they were the only two people in the world. Jonathon Townsend had asked to escort her to the ball. The giddiness of that thought forced an unbidden grin on her face. She must calm down or she'd surely look like a Cheshire cat. Now what was she about to do?

Mary! How long had she been waiting? Lettie hurried back inside and found Mary still looking at the photos. "I'm so sorry. I didn't mean to make you wait so long."

Mary lifted an eyebrow. "It hasn't been that long, truly."

"Oh, it seemed like it was." Lettie glanced at the wall. "Do you like the photos?"

"Yes. You did an excellent job taking them. Everyone has been commenting about them. Of course, I don't care for the ones I'm in."

"Don't be silly. You look wonderful."

"I particularly like the photos you took of Miss Dupont." Mary pointed to several photos of the woman.

"I certainly took a lot of them, per her request."

"She does like the attention."

"What do you think of Mr. Honeywell?" Lettie wondered if Mary had the same reaction to the man that she did.

"I like his English accent. Why?"

"I was just wondering." She took Mary's arm. "Well, let's go. We have time before the next presentation."

"Your aunt won't mind?"

"No, she won't. If she has one of her headaches, she'll be in her room, so we'll be quiet."

They hurried down the street, discussing the lectures and comparing the presenters they'd heard. When they reached Aunt Gertie's house, Lettie opened the door quietly. She motioned Mary inside, and Lettie put a finger to her lips.

"She must be taking a nap," Lettie whispered. She motioned Mary to follow and led the young woman to her room. Inside her room, Lettie went to the closet and opened it, perusing its contents. She selected three dresses—a pale blue, a yellow one, and a pink one—and laid them out on the bed. "I believe all of these will fit you. They're my church dresses and are quite appropriate for you to wear to the ball. Which one would you like to wear?"

Mary's mouth gaped. "You're letting me borrow one of your dresses?" Her eyes glistened. "Are you sure?"

"Absolutely. I want you to enjoy the ball."

Mary fingered the material of each dress, stroking the satin sashes. "Oh, they're all so pretty."

"Well, I'd let you take all three, but you can only wear one to the ball."

Mary gave a timid smile. "I've always liked blue, so I'll take that one." She pointed to the blue dress. "Are you sure it'll fit?"

Lettie held the dress up to Mary. "Yes, I think so. You're so tiny, you might want to pull the sash more tightly, but I think it'll be lovely on you."

Mary clasped the dress to her. "I may not look pretty, but I'll sure feel pretty!"

"You *will* be pretty. Pretty outside as you are inside."

"How can I ever thank you?"

"You already have by letting me do this for you."

Chapter Ten

Jonathon hadn't been so excited since he was ten years old and got a pony for Christmas. But this time, he would be the giver and not the recipient. He couldn't wait to see Lettie's reaction and hoped her response would be what he desired. But first, the ball.

As he drove the Pierce Arrow to her aunt's house, he practiced what he wanted to say to her when the right time came. He parked the car in front, then climbed out and straightened his tuxedo and adjusted his cravat. Her aunt had hinted about her gorgeous dress, so he wanted to be suitably attired as her escort. He chuckled to himself. Her aunt had also helped him with the ruse he'd engineered.

At first, he'd been worried about Caroline's reaction to his being with Lettie, but Mother had told him a fellow traveler Caroline met on their cruise had written her and planned to visit. Apparently, Caroline was more interested in pursuing a future with that man than hoping for one with Jonathon. *Thank you, God.* After all, he hadn't intended to hurt Caroline's feelings, but wanted to be honest about his.

Jonathon jogged up the front steps of Tranquility Cottage and rapped on the door. Gertrude Ross opened it. "Good evening, Jonathon! My, don't you look dapper?"

"Thank you, Mrs. Ross."

"Still having trouble with those snakes?" Her eyes

twinkled.

"I believe we've finally gotten rid of them." He winked at her, then froze at the breathtaking vision that stepped into the room. His heart leaped with pleasure as Lettie walked toward him.

"Good evening, Jonathon." Her smile dazzled, drawing his eyes away from the elegant crimson dress accented with black lace that perfectly draped her form.

He took her extended hand and kissed the back of it. "Good evening, Lettie. You look absolutely stunning, beautiful."

"Thank you." She accepted the black gloves from her aunt and pulled them on, then took the black lace shawl and allowed Jonathon to drape it over her shoulders. He hoped she didn't notice his hands shaking in the process, but the touch of her skin against his hands took his breath away.

He turned to her aunt. "Are you certain you don't wish to go to the ball and celebrate the holiday?"

She shook her head. "No, thank you, Jonathon. I'll save my celebrating for later." She gave him a meaningful glance. "For now, I'd like to rest and listen to my Victrola. You two go on and have a wonderful evening."

"That we will." He opened the door for Lettie to exit. "Good night."

"Good night, Aunt Gertie," Lettie said.

Jonathon could barely keep his eyes on the road on the way to the ball. He just wanted to look at Lettie, to soak in her beauty. When they arrived at the main hall of the Assembly that had been transformed into a ballroom, all eyes were on them. His heart swelled with pride as he walked in with her on his arm. He was certain there wasn't another woman in the room as beautiful as Lettie, and probably not even in the world, as far as he was concerned.

When the orchestra began playing, he took her in his arms, and they glided across the floor in perfect harmony. They gazed into each other's face, their eyes speaking volumes they hadn't yet expressed. Lettie glanced away to watch the other dancers.

"There's Mary!"

Jonathon followed her gaze, recognizing the young women he'd seen with Lettie.

"Doesn't she look lovely?" Lettie gave a little wave, and the other woman smiled and waved back, right as she began to dance with a young man.

"She does, but nowhere near as lovely as you," Jonathon said.

"You told Aunt Gertie the snakes are gone. So it's safe to go back there now? You definitely have the best location on the lake because you can see everything from there—the church, the Assembly Hall, the hotel. It would be a shame if it were unsafe to go down to the water."

"Yes, it's safe now. Perhaps you and I can take a stroll over there afterwards. It's a full moon which makes the lake so beautiful."

"Tonight? That sounds lovely."

Lettie wanted to pinch herself to make sure she wasn't dreaming. She was in a fairy tale dancing with her Prince Charming. Her heart almost burst with happiness being in his arms. Surely, they were the most perfect couple at the ball. She breathed a prayer of thanksgiving to God for allowing her to accompany Aunt Gertie and therefore meet Jonathon.

Across the room, Helene Dupont danced with Baxter Honeywell. As was their style, the two demanded attention with their exaggerated dance moves. Miss Dupont's form-fitting dress only allowed movement from the knees down, where layers of ruffles cascaded to the floor. A diamond necklace sparkled from the expanse of skin from her neck to her low-cut bodice. When Miss Dupont caught Lettie's eye, she winked and smiled.

Jonathon followed her gaze. "I see you've made friends with Miss Dupont."

"Acquaintances, I'd say. I don't really feel that I know her. I feel like I know the person she wants me to know, but maybe not who she really is."

His eyebrows lifted. "In other words, you know the actress, but maybe not the real person inside the actress."

"Exactly. It seems that she is always performing, although she was almost sincere when we had tea together. But Mr. Honeywell is a mystery to me. He appears to be nice on the outside, but sinister on the inside."

"I suppose it's your photographer's eye that sees more than the average person sees."

"Thank you, Jonathon, for saying that. I do believe I'm more observant than most people."

"I know everyone has enjoyed seeing the pictures you've taken."

"Yes, I'm very pleased with the response. It's what I had hoped for. I wanted the photos to be of benefit somehow."

Mary approached them, a worried look on her face.

"Please excuse me for interrupting you," she said.

"Mary, you look lovely, but what's wrong?"

"Something's been bothering me, and I think I know what it is. Can you come with me?"

Lettie glanced at Jonathon. "Of course, but please come back," he said.

"No, you come too, Mr. Townsend."

They followed Mary to the lobby of the building where the photographs were displayed. She walked over to a photo of Miss Dupont and pointed. "See there? See that birthmark on her neck?"

"Yes, I noticed it when I took the pictures. I believe her hair covers it most the time. Why?"

"When you asked me to describe the robber, I knew

there was something I noticed but forgot to mention. He had a birthmark on his neck, just like that one."

Jonathon and Lettie exchanged glances.

"Jonathon, do you think she could be the robber?" Lettie asked.

"She's certainly tall, but she doesn't look like a man."

"But she could. She has plenty of costumes, plus she's an actress and can play the part," Lettie said.

"And remember how she could change her voice on stage?" Mary said. "She could sing low as well as high."

"You know I had my suspicions about Mr. Honeywell, but he was accounted for. I bet they staged the whole scene," Lettie said. "What should we do?"

Jonathon looked over at the two Pinkerton guards standing near the door. "We'll tell them. They will notify the other guards to make sure Miss Dupont and Mr. Honeywell don't get away." Jonathon approached the guards, telling them their suspicions, then he returned to the women.

"What shall we do in the meantime?" Mary asked. "We don't want them to think we suspect them."

"Let's go back inside and act as if we're unaware. Just don't look at them," Jonathon said.

The three re-entered the ballroom and went to the punch table where they each picked up a punch cup and sipped. The two guards Jonathon had spoken with crossed the room and spoke to the guards by the doors on the opposite side as Lettie, Jonathon, and Mary watched out of the corners of their eyes. A few moments later, Mr. Honeywell's voice rose above the music. "See here, now. What's the meaning of this?"

All eyes looked toward him where two of the guards held each of his arms. Ladies gasped as the other two guards took Miss Dupont's arms and led the couple out.

"Well, now, it seems we are rid of two more snakes," Jonathon said.

Lettie tried to smile, but she wasn't happy to discover

Miss Dupont had been pretending all along. "I feel sorry for her."

"You wanted to believe she was a better person than that, which is one of the things I admire about you. You're always looking for the best in people."

"It's true," Mary said. "Lettie, you've been such a blessing to me."

Lettie's face warmed. "But Mary, you're the one who solved the mystery. Perhaps you should become a Pinkerton agent!"

"Me? A woman?"

"That's not such a strange idea. Actually, Pinkerton does have women agents," Jonathon said. "Maybe you should apply."

Mary shook her head. "No, thank you. I plan to use my detective skills in the classroom when I have to find out who put the frog in Susie's lunch pail."

Jonathon and Lettie laughed, and Lettie gave Mary a hug.

Jonathon took Lettie's arm. "Would you please excuse us, Mary? I promised this lady a walk in the moonlight."

Jonathon led Lettie outside where the brilliant moon lit their surroundings in an ethereal glow. She tucked her hand in the crook of his arm as they strolled down to the lake.

"It's so beautiful tonight. The moonlight casts a sheen on the water and creates a path one might be tempted to walk on."

"We'll leave that to the snakes," he said.

"I'm glad we don't have to worry about them."

"Close your eyes."

"What? Why?"

"Close your eyes. Trust me, I won't let you fall." Jonathon tightened his grip on her arm.

She did as he asked and allowed him to lead her a ways farther. "Jonathon, what are you doing?"

They stopped. "Okay, you may open your eyes now."

When Lettie did, she discovered they were standing in front of a beautiful gazebo decorated with Christmas garland and red velvet bows, built over the edge of the water. Her mouth fell open as she looked around and discovered it was behind Jonathon's house.

"Jonathon! This is lovely!"

"Please join me inside." He took her hand and led her up the two steps into the octagonal building. They walked to the railing beside the water and gazed out. The night air was punctuated by owl hoots and occasional goose honks.

"It's so peaceful here." She turned to look up at him. "There weren't any snakes, were there?"

He gazed down at her. "No, but I had to think of something to keep you away while it was being built so I could surprise you with it."

"You built this for me? But why?"

He clasped her hands. "It's my Christmas gift to you. You mentioned that we needed something by the lake so we could enjoy being near the water."

"But Jonathon. This is your land, not mine."

"I was hoping the gazebo might entice you to stay here longer."

"Oh? And why would I want to do that?"

He leaned down and kissed her, releasing emotions she'd held back. As he pulled her close, she let her senses fully entwine with his and absorb the love the kiss conveyed. When the kiss ended, she caught her breath as his gaze penetrated hers.

"I love you, Lettie Morgan. And I think you love me too. Is that a good enough reason to stay?"

"Hmm. I don't know which is the better Christmas gift—the gazebo or you."

"Take your time to answer that question, a lifetime."

The End

A "literary archaeologist," Marilyn Turk writes historical fiction flavored with suspense and romance for Barbour Books, Winged Publications and Lighthouse Publishing of the Carolinas. One of her World War II novels, *The Gilded Curse*, won a Silver Scroll award. She has also written a series of novels set in 1800 Florida whose settings are lighthouses. In addition, Marilyn's novellas have been published in the Great Lakes Lighthouse Brides collection and Crinoline Cowboys. Marilyn also writes for Guideposts magazine and Daily Guideposts Devotions. She is a member of American Christian Fiction Writers, Romance Writers of America, Advanced Writers and Speakers Association and Word Weavers International.

When not writing, Marilyn and her husband enjoy boating, fishing, playing tennis or visiting lighthouses.

Marilyn is a regular contributor to the Heroes, Heroines and History blog. https://www.hhhistory.com). Connect with her at http://pathwayheart.com,
https://twitter.com/MarilynTurk,
https://www.facebook.com/MarilynTurkAuthor/,
https://www.pinterest.com/bluewaterbayou/,
marilynturkwriter@yahoo.com.

The Christmas Surprise
By Lenora Worth

Chapter One

Present Day

Jon Townsend stood at the window of his second-story office and watched the woman pacing back and forth on the lake path near the old gazebo, a nice distraction from the estate papers he'd been working on all morning. Being a lawyer in a small town required a lot of coffee at times. The work of estates and a last will and testament could become very boring, very quickly. This morning, he'd been trying to figure out how to convince Mrs. Montgomery to reconsider leaving her millions to her six cats. Her only child, a dedicated son who sold enough real estate to make a good living, had held off on marriage because of love and fear of his strongly opinionated mother. Quincy had finally found true love when he'd met a single woman from Orlando who wanted to escape the city and live in a small artsy-type town.

Mrs. Montgomery didn't approve of the person he wanted to marry because Mrs. Montgomery didn't know *her people*, so she'd decided to disown Marcus. Who would look after the cats if she did that?

Putting that dilemma out of his mind, Jon watched the woman walking along the old footpath that circled the lake. The original path, started well over a century ago, had encompassed beaten down leaves and a dirt trail. About twenty years ago the path had been asphalted and was now wide enough for bikers to pass joggers, and skateboarders to avoid scooter chairs and baby strollers. The trail made a nice tree-shaded outdoor space that tourists, townsfolk, and homeowners mutually enjoyed. Jon often walked it early in the morning, stopping to visit with neighbors along the way. But he didn't recognize the woman below who paced more than she actually walked.

He had to admit, as distractions went, she was a beauty. A cold December wind played with her shoulder-length strawberry blonde hair and whipped against her fitted tan coat. She wore buttery-brown boots and dark stockings under a pleated black skirt and carried a tote bag that had to be heavy since it looked stuffed to the gills with papers shooting out like white duck feathers.

She shouldered the bag while she ranted into her cell phone, using her free hand for emphasis, her voice carrying but not enough for him to hear what she was discussing.

She wasn't watching where she was headed, which was perilously close to the flock of Canadian geese that had taken up permanent residence in Springlake, Florida. The mild Panhandle weather seemed to agree with the ornery birds.

They didn't like humans invading their property. She didn't have a clue that she was about to be hissed at and slapped with a feathered wing or two, or, worse, charged and chased by the whole flock.

Jon took it upon himself to save this damsel before a rogue goose flew up into her pretty face and caused her to drop her precious phone into the cold lake.

He hurried down the creaky yet still-grand staircase of the old Victorian house that had belonged to his family since the late eighteen-hundreds. His family had founded Springlake and built Magnolia Manor on the lake. Every window on the back of this rambling house, including the turret room on the third floor, had a lovely view of the naturally oval, spring-feed lake around which the entire community revolved.

Jon rushed down the hall and hit the ornate, rounded second-floor landing that showcased a tall stained-glass window. When he reached the wide front foyer, he skidded past the antique Chippendale sideboard that stood outside the formal dining room to head to the back entry of the first floor. Then he opened the double stained-glass doors that matched the front doors of the house and stepped onto the wide wraparound porch next to the sunroom. She was still there and the geese were beginning to squawk. Was the she oblivious to the world around her?

He crossed the wide, sloping yard and charged down the worn brick steps toward the old gazebo that the church ladies still wanted to decorate at Christmas. But the weathered gazebo had become worn and brittle, like his attitude. He'd asked them to leave it alone because one of them could get hurt or, worse, fall into the lake and drown.

A gust of winter wind hit the air and caused old leaves to dance up and swirl around in a flurry. At about that time, she glanced up and into the charging hiss of an angry goose with an outstretched neck and a noisy agitation.

"Hey," Jon called, running now.

The woman waved her phone at the goose and glanced back at Jon. "Go away! Now!"

Not sure she was talking to him or the goose, Jon sprinted toward her. "That won't work," he called as he reached her, out of breath.

The goose advanced. The woman stepped back.

Jon had no choice but to grab her up and out of the way of the flapping, flying goose.

That didn't go very well. The woman was now flapping to get away from him.

"Let me go," she said, glaring at him over her shoulder. "I know how to deal with a wild goose."

When the goose came closer and snarled a squawking

retort, Miss Brave turned and shuddered in Jon's arms.

"Allow me," Jon said with a tone of sarcasm, disengaging himself from her dainty arms. Then he turned, releasing her, and shouted and shooed at the goose. "Lucy, go away. You don't have babies anymore. They all flew the nest."

The goose hissed at Jon then turned and ran in the other direction. When the whole flock sensed a tiny dog walking with his owner, they all followed Lucy to the lake.

That left an awkward silence between Jon and the woman holding onto her phone and her bag for dear life, her blue-green eyes wide against her heart-shaped, shocked face.

Jon studied her up close. She had a cute nose with freckles sprinkled like cinnamon across it and nice, full lips that went with that heart-shaped face. Her eyes held a hint of how-dare-you, coupled with who-are-you.

So much more intriguing than dealing with Mr. Pepperidge's seventeen grandchildren and the trust funds he wanted to leave each of them. That had been next on Jon's list, but it could wait for a while since he had a meeting to attend in a few minutes. Mr. Pepperidge changed his mind and his will at least three times a year anyway.

"Thank you, I think," she said, now back to being haughty and all business. The chilly wind kept blowing one wild curl across her face. Then she added, "It's goslings. A baby goose is a gosling."

"You're welcome, I think," he replied, his hands in the pocket of his jeans. "Sorry I didn't have time for the correct term to scream at a goose. I was busy trying to keep feathers from flying."

Now that he was close to her, Jon's shyness crept up inside him and he wasn't sure what to do next. No wonder he was still single, in spite of the available women who baked him cookies and casseroles on a regular basis and just happened to be in the neighborhood.

She gave him a measured stare then glanced around. "I

didn't see that thing coming. I didn't even see the geese."

"Hard to miss." He smiled at the gathering of geese down on the shore and then gazed at her. "I'm thinking you're not from around these parts, are you?"

She laughed at that. "No, I'm from Atlanta. I'm here on business." She glanced at her watch. "And I'm late." She whirled in the same way the leaves did and smiled at him. "Thank you for rescuing me from Lucy."

"You're welcome." Jon checked his watch. "I have a meeting myself. I'd better get going, too."

She nodded and turned to make her way along the path. Since he didn't see a car, Jon wondered if she was here for a day or if she might be staying in the historic Springlake Hotel. That's where he was headed. Maybe he'd run into her again.

Then he realized he hadn't introduced himself.

But then, neither had she.

Lynsey Milton hurried up the steps to the Springlake Hotel and tried to get her mind back on the meeting about to take place instead of thinking about the man she'd come across on the lake path. Tall and shy, good-looking in that goofy boy-next-door way, he sure was a heroic goose chaser. That made her smile. Oh, well, she didn't know if she'd ever see him again, but if this meeting went as planned, she might get to stick around. Who knew?

This could be a good day for Springlake, Florida to become viable and thriving again. The Restoration Committee had worked hard to bring this together. After the phone call she'd just received from her boss, Lynsey felt the pressure even more. She'd get a promotion if the town voted in favor of the restoration. If she didn't win them over, she'd probably be out of a job. Since she loved her job, she aimed to put on the Southern charm.

After all, her mama had raised her with not only proper manners but also with good common sense. That and a degree in Business Administration from the University of Georgia gave her the confidence she needed to get this project going. She hoped.

Lately, it seemed everything she'd tried career-wise had gone terribly wrong. Two big projects in Georgia had fallen through over the last year. And so had her love life. Maybe the third time would be the charm, at least with her career. She needed this one to work.

Restoring towns to their former glory could be a hard task. Some wanted progression all the way even if it meant tearing down old historical buildings and putting in strip malls. They believed in progress and going all-out modern, which was needed at times but not in Springlake. Located in the Panhandle of Florida, it had a distinct history full of intriguing, interesting people. Built around the springs it had weathered fires, storms, and turbulent times, and it was only an hour or so away from the Gulf and held small town charm while still being very convenient for tourists.

Thankfully, some of the leaders of Springlake had thought better of tearing down and starting over. They wanted progress, but they also wanted to preserve the past in a quaint way. And that's where Lynsey came in.

Lynsey was a specialist on revitalizing fading little towns and this one was a gem. A diamond in the rough that needed to be renovated and restored into not only a thriving tourist mecca, and a good place to live and raise a family.

Now she had to convince the rest of them that restoration was a good idea. Today was the preliminary meeting of the restoration committee.

But when she walked into the elegant meeting room that held the charm she'd first noticed in Springlake and saw the man standing with some of the committee members, her confident mood skidded to a stop and her heart beat even faster.

The man who'd saved her from tangling with a goose stood at the head of the room with several of the people in charge. Was he on her list of people to woo? He must live on the lake since he'd seen her on the path. She'd been so busy with the details of her presentation she had yet to memorize all of the names and positions of the appointed committee members. The head of the committee had abruptly resigned before Lynsey had even had a chance to meet with her. She'd learn today who'd taken her place.

The room was getting crowded since everyone had an opinion on how this should go. Obviously her new hero had a reason for showing up.

Lynsey stopped and held her breath. He was cute. Good-looking and very self-assured, he wore the same clothes he'd had on earlier, jeans and a gray V-neck sweater over a button-up blue shirt that matched his dark blue eyes. His curly brown hair was scattered across his forehead in defiance, which only made him more interesting. Then she noticed his feet. Sneakers at a town meeting? And plaid at that? How had she missed that detail earlier?

He had to be a bit eccentric to break the stuffed-shirt mold. She liked him immediately. Then Lynsey blinked and tried to focus. Maybe he *was* just an interested citizen. Taking a breath, she thought over her notes and research. She was ready.

As she started up the aisle, he looked around and into her eyes then smiled a big, surprised smile that only made him more handsome.

Lynsey took another calming breath. This should be interesting. It had been a long time since she'd really noticed a man, let alone think about one in any kind of romantic way. Too many bad first dates and stalled-out relationships had broken her.

But this one had her full attention. He'd saved her from being mauled by an angry, territorial goose named Lucy.

Telling herself to behave and get her mind back on business, Lynsey dismissed the surge of longing moving over her.

He might seem like hero material only she didn't really know him.

She did wonder what part he'd play in this meeting.

Chapter Two

Well, this meeting might actually be interesting.

Jon nodded to the woman walking up the aisle. Before he could make a move to introduce himself, Mayor Kathryn Barton pushed past him, leaving a wisp of gardenia-inspired perfume trailing right into his nose.

While Jon tried not to sneeze, the mayor turned on the charm. "Lynsey, it's so good to see you again. Did you get all settled in? My assistant booked you into the best suite."

The young woman shook the mayor's hand and gave her a sheepish smile. "Yes, Mayor Barton. The suite is beautiful. The hotel is amazing, too. I love the atrium ceiling in the lobby and the original furnishings in all of the rooms, including this one."

Jon couldn't argue with that. The brick hotel with the famous octagon-shaped bridal suite on the third floor sat on a corner of the main street through town, where several of the older buildings had either been shut down or turned into antique malls and flea markets. Main Street needed a facelift but he was afraid this supercharged committee would go overboard, and he had a bad feeling this interesting woman might be involved in that plan.

"Good. That's good to hear." The beaming mayor turned to smile at Jon and the committee gathering at the head table. "Have you met everyone?"

Lynsey, as the mayor had called her, glanced at the three other people who'd made their way to the front of the small, stately conference room. "I think so. Of course, I've met Mr. Hampton, the hotel manager."

Ned Hampton, looking as debonair as always with his horn-rimmed glasses and red bow tie, shook her hand. "So happy you're here, Lynsey. Call me Ned."

"Thank you, Ned." Lynsey went on to smile at the tall, slender woman who stood next to Ned. "Mrs. Scott. High school English, one of my favorite subjects. I hear you're also the local historian. We didn't get to discuss that when we met earlier."

"No, we didn't," Stella Scott said, for once not looking down her nose. Clutching her pearls, she added, "I've heard so many wonderful things about you, Miss Milton."

"Lynsey. Please call me Lynsey."

Lynsey moved to the next person. "And Mr. Norton is the city planner."

Wendell Norton pumped Lynsey's small hand, his hazel eyes roaming over her face. "We'll be working closely together."

Jon didn't like the leer on Wendell's face. The man was a player. He'd probably ask her out on a date before they ever got through the planning meeting. Jon had gone to high school and college with Wendell, so he knew it to be true.

Then she glanced at Jon, her expression playful now. "I didn't get your name."

The mayor glowered at Jon, her pink lips petulant. "You didn't introduce yourself, Jon Townsend? Where are your manners?"

"I ... uh...," Jon never stuttered but the mayor had been his Sunday school teacher when he was eight and had forced him to learn several Bible verses each time he acted out. She still frightened him but he was determined to be assertive with her. Even though he did still remember those verses.

"It's my fault," Lynsey said, shaking her head. "I walked

into a flock of geese by the lake and, well, Lucy didn't like me being in her territory."

Everyone but the mayor chuckled. While Mayor Barton looked shocked, Stella said, "Lucy is a pain. But we tolerate her anyway." She eyed the mayor, however, when she emphasized putting up with pains.

Jon nodded, thankful for the save. "I happened by and shooed Lucy away and then we both realized we were late." He shrugged. "And here we are."

"I had no idea we were headed for the same meeting," Lynsey said, giving him a questioning look. "We could have walked over together."

"Neither did I or I would have enjoyed escorting you to the meeting." Holding out his hand to Lynsey, he said, "Hi. I'm Jon Townsend."

Her eyes widened as realization hit her. "Of *the* Townsends?"

Mayor Barton beamed a hundred-watt smile. "Great-great-great-grandson. I think there might be one or two more *greats* in there, but, honestly, I can't keep count."

Stella did an eye roll. "Kathryn, you need to learn the history of the town since you *are* mayor. Jonathan is a sixth-generation Townsend."

Mayor Barton waved her hand in the air, her bangle rattling down her arm. "I know my history well enough, Stella. He's a Townsend and that's all we need to know."

"I am of *the* Townsends," Jon replied with a grin to Lynsey. "Can't seem to shake 'em."

"I'm Lynsey Milton," the woman replied. "I'm so sorry I didn't tell you my name earlier." Giving him a quizzical stare, she said, "I understand your family helped bring the railroad and that's when your ancestor discovered the lake and founded the town."

"He did, indeed," Jon replied, used to people asking about his prominent family. "And we stayed. Well, most of us stayed. I came back a few years ago and I guess I'm here to stay."

"Well, now you know everyone," the mayor said to Lynsey on an impatient note. "Let's get started, shall we?"

Lynsey moved closer to Jon. "Are you on the planning committee?"

Jon nodded. "Somehow, I've become the chairman of the planning committee."

"I was told no one from the founding family was available," she replied, confusion coloring her eyes. "I wish I'd known sooner. I have a lot of questions."

"I had told everyone I didn't want to be on the committee," he admitted. "My housekeeper-slash-self-appointed-assistant Ethel convinced me I needed to be part of this after the last chairman ran away with her hands in the air. The person before her only lasted a week and I'm pretty sure he's moving his family to Destin now."

Lynsey shook her head at that and smiled at him. "I have to admit, I was expecting someone old and doddering."

Jon scratched his head. "I'm getting older by the minute and I can be doddering at times. Especially at times like this when I get overly agitated."

"Why did you hesitate?" she asked as they moved toward their seats. "Shouldn't you have been part of this from the beginning?"

Jon stifled his doubts and said, "I declined because I don't want our town to change too much. I'm kind of old-fashioned in that way. I like it the way it is."

"All the more reason you should be on the committee," Lynsey whispered. "You can keep this town restoration on track."

"I'm not sure anyone can do that," he admitted, feeling better after earlier when he'd begun to believe she might be the enemy. "You've met the other committee members. Didn't you see the glee in their eyes?"

"Let's talk about things and we'll take care of too much glee," she said. Then she gave him another smile. "After all, you did ward off Lucy. Surely you can handle this group."

Jon decided he liked Lynsey Milton. Maybe she was right. Rather than shying away from changing the town his ancestors had founded, he should embrace this and work to make it better. He'd always wanted Springlake to stay viable and strong. He'd returned home a few years ago when his father had become ill and had stayed after he died. Now life and small-town law took up most of his time. His days went by in a haze of corporate and estate laws, but most of the town depended on him when it came to any changes. He wasn't so sure he wanted to be the bearer of that burden.

Well, now it was happening. But he still didn't understand where she came in.

"And why are you here?" he asked, wondering what she had to do with all of this.

"I'm the project manager," she said. "I work for Heritage Restorations. I'm here to guide all of you through the process."

Shocked, he had to chuckle. "That's funny, since I was expecting someone older and stuffier.

"I'm old enough," she said, giving him a wry smile. "Trust me. I'm not the stuffy kind."

Jon's heart did a bump while his head told him to turn and head out the door. He'd left Tallahassee to come home, more to the story than just returning to his hometown to take over things for his ailing father.

He'd left because he'd broken up with an ambitious, determined woman who wanted to change him way too much.

He wouldn't fall for that again.

Especially not when it involved the town his family had put on the map.

"So how did I do?" Lynsey didn't know why it was so important to her that Jon approved her PowerPoint presentation. She'd always given talks to an audience of one. Find one person in the room and glance at that person a lot to keep calm and focused.

He had become that person today. Now she wished she'd focused more on Stella Scott or Wendell Norton. But Wendell seemed a bit too focused on her, so she didn't want to give him the wrong idea and Stella's expressions were hard to read. Ned Hampton had been called out on a hotel matter. So that left Jon alone with the roomful of citizens who'd come to voice their pros and cons.

Jon presented a solid, calm front even if he was gun-shy on getting involved. His name and the legacy of his ancestors carried a lot of weight, so she was glad he'd come on board.

He'd been the one who seemed the most relaxed when she'd clicked on the preliminary drawings. "This could be the new and improved Springlake," she said, waiting for the reaction. Some people nodded and smiled. Other listened with cynical faces as she talked about retail boutiques, coffee shops, and a variety of restaurants. "And we'll do a total overhaul with landscaping. Palm trees and colorful dish gardens with a variety of local flora and fauna. The whole façade will look old, but your main street will be thoroughly modern and welcoming."

Now they were having lunch with the other committee members in a private room with a lake view. The Queen Anne table centered in the room held two bright green Royal Worcester vases etched in gold.

"You did great," Jon replied. Then he took a sip of coffee from a delicate white china cup rimmed with gold. "I'm learning so much about critical mass and specialty retail."

"I'm sure you've heard those terms before," she replied, noticing the way he crinkled his brow when he looked confused. "The mayor made it a point to tell me you're a lawyer." Leaning in, she added, "A Yale-educated one at that."

He gave her a fleeting frown followed by a shrug. "I could be working at the fancy firm I started with in Tallahassee, but coming home was both a duty and a necessity. As far as Yale, I had no choice. A family tradition. I mostly deal in estate law and small claims court. A different kind of critical mass. A lot of family drama and dysfunction, but, hey, it pays the bills."

Lynsey could imagine him pouring over legalese. "You're still not sure about creating a vibrant downtown for Springlake, are you?"

Jon studied her face, his expression hard to read. He had a noble presence that added to his old-fashioned charm. "I don't think we qualify for a downtown. We're a *small* town. I'd like to keep the plans on a small scale."

"You think the mayor and her cronies are biting off more than they can chew?"

He laughed at that. "Well, maybe. You presented a convincing streetscape of restaurants, retail shops and other business establishments. I like the idea of a new performing arts center and we need more office space. I worry that we don't have the population or the location for some of the more radical changes." He glanced out the window. "We're not exactly a resort destination like we were in the old days."

"So you don't believe in 'if we build it, they will come'?"

"Ah, *Field of Dreams*. I loved that movie," he admitted. "Only it was a fantasy. I have to deal in reality."

"Why did they pick you to head the committee since you said two others came before you?"

"I was the last person standing, I think. So duty calls, as always."

"You'll need to be tough on them."

His brow furrowed. "What if I can't? I'm tough in a

court of law, but I have to carry on the family reputation and that means I try to get along with everyone."

"You have to decide what's best for Springlake. Can you do that?"

"I think you're the tough one," he said, acutely aware of her being the adorable one, too. "Want me to step down already?"

"No. I want you to stay and be part of the solution." Lynsey had listened to Jon in the meeting. He had asked all the right questions and he'd fielded the tough crowd which seemed divided about what to do next. He had the grace and calmness needed in a court of law and also in a town meeting. He could be a valuable ally. Or her worst enemy.

"I got roped into this," he said, giving the others who sat chattering on the other side of the table a long stare. "The mayor means well but she gets overenthusiastic without thinking things through, and Wendell will follow her lead because he has a nose for making money at any cost."

"You mean he suffers from a tad of greed?"

"Did it show in my face or my words?"

"Both," she replied in a whisper. "But it showed more coming from him so I'd already pegged him on that."

"Well, he has other qualities you might need to peg, too."

"Duly noted." Lynsey went back to business. "You realize a vibrant downtown can bring in new real estate and new businesses. The arts and festivals draw big crowds and they notice things. They'll see our quality of life and want to move here. They'd be willing to commute to work in the surrounding larger cities."

"Or they might just decide to live in those surrounding large cities."

"That's why we need to entice them with updated facades and authentic historical buildings. A real cityscape will make them love everything about this place. You have the beautiful spring-fed lake for boating, kayaking and paddle-boarding. So many fun outdoor activities for tourists and townsfolk alike, and more walking trails and adventurous activities. Why not show that off?"

"Maybe I like the quiet."

"Maybe quiet only means this town is dying a slow death."

She saw the doubt in his eyes but he recovered and gave her a bland expression. "I have a lot to think about." He stood, obviously done with not only his banana pudding, and with her, too. "I have to get back to my real job."

"Before you go," Lynsey said, standing too, "would you be willing to give me a tour of your home? This morning I walked down to the lake to get my first glimpse. Then my boss called and, well, you know the rest. Seeing the interior will help me get a handle on how to go about building the design for the town proper."

He hesitated, looked out at the lake, and then finally nodded. "I could do that sometime tomorrow. How 'bout around four o'clock?"

"I'll be there," she said, wondering if she'd already overstepped and messed things up.

"I'll see you then," he said. "It was nice to meet you, Lynsey."

He nodded at the others and left.

Wendell came over to where Lynsey stood staring. "Always a moody one. Jon and I have known each other since kindergarten. Went to high school and college together. Never could figure him out."

"He seems nice enough," Lynsey said in Jon's defense.

"He's nice, all right. Too nice at times," Wendell replied with a sneer. "Hey, why don't we go find a drink and get to know each other better?"

Lynsey held the eye roll she so wanted to give him. "I have to get to work and then I have plans later." She didn't tell those plans involved charts and graphs.

"Too bad." Wendell turned and exited.

Mayor Barton came up, her pink sweater shining like a neon light. "I thought that went rather well, didn't it?"

"I think we had a good turnout for the meeting," Lynsey said. "We still have a lot of work to do to convince people to back this. Some towns don't like change."

"But some mayors do," Kathryn said with a sweet smile. "I happen to be one of those. We want to take a vote before Christmas, so we need to keep at it."

Lynsey gathered her things and bid good day to the remaining people who'd been invited to the private luncheon, the baked chicken and shrimp salad sitting heavy in her stomach. She refused to be anxious about this. She'd done this before and faced a lot of opposition but always managed to get the job done.

Now she had to wonder if she'd finally met her match in Jon Townsend.

He came from the family who'd created this town. He didn't like change. He appeared a bit melancholy. What was she missing? He also seemed to especially not like people such as her—an outsider coming in to boss everyone around.

Was that how he saw her? And if so, why did that concern her more than anything else she had to think about?

Chapter Three

The next afternoon, Jon finished his work and closed down his laptop. Thankfully, Mrs. Montgomery had seen the light about leaving her fortune to her cats. After Jon had fully vetted Earlene Rackley's family tree and told Virginia Montgomery that Earlene's people had a lot of money, too, and that her uncle had once served as a state senator, Virginia warmed up to her future daughter-in-law.

"Well, she dresses a bit too flashy for my taste and she comes from Orlando, of all places," Virginia had explained over the phone. "But she does make my Quincy happy. And if I'm to ever get any grandchildren, I guess I can live with her. Besides, Quincy threatened to move out of the house if I didn't accept her! Can you imagine? I'm still leaving my darlings a trust fund."

"Your darlings will appreciate that, and I know Quincy will appreciate your blessings," Jon had told Virginia, thinking her lakeside mansion might not be big enough for two women in Quincy's life. He might have to find his bride her own domain. "And please consider when he marries Earlene you might get those grandchildren and they'll become your darlings immediately."

Virginia let out a long-suffering sigh. "I should set up a trust for them one day, too?"

"Exactly."

Jon leaned back in his chair and placed his hands behind his head. He'd started the process of setting up trust funds for Harold Pepperidge's grandchildren, glad all the elderly wealthy people around town depended on his expertise and trusted him with handling their wills. He gave out advice along with strategy, it seemed. All in all, a good day's work.

Ethel came in and put her hands on her ample hips, her white blouse and navy skirt as crisp as they'd been this morning. "Don't get too comfortable. Your four o'clock is on her way, according to my sources."

Jon dropped his arms and immediately stood, knocking his chair into a spin. Lynsey Milton. He'd thought about her a lot but had forgotten she was coming to tour the house today. "She can't be early. I didn't notice the time."

"Go," Ethel, sixty-eight and spry, said as she pushed him toward the half-bath in his office. "You have about fifteen minutes. The mayor's secretary reported that Lynsey left the mayor's office about twenty minutes ago to return to the hotel. If she arrives before you're ready, I'll stall her with historical facts."

"Great idea." Jon left the door open while he combed his hair. Ethel also volunteered at the welcome center down the street and loved to talk about the history of Springlake. "And tell her I'll be right there even if I'm not actually right there."

Ethel adjusted her bifocals, used to him running late. "There's an Italian casserole in the refrigerator with instructions on how to heat it. A salad is ready, and the rolls are on the stove."

"Thank you, Ethel."

"Oh, and fresh cookies on the counter."

"I don't deserve you," he said while he tried to brush his teeth.

"I know," Ethel replied tartly. His all-around helper and friend pushed at her short gray hair and smiled at his deep appreciation. "Oh, and I made enough food for two."

Jon groaned while Ethel scooted out the office door before he could protest. Why did she and everyone else around here always try to play matchmaker for him?

She cares about you, he reminded himself. Else she would have retired a long time ago. She kind of came with the house when he'd inherited it.

He was an orphan of sorts. The last man standing in a long line of Townsends after his father had died five years ago. Jon had lost his mother when he was in high school and since his father had never remarried, he had no siblings. The community wanted him to marry and bear children to keep the name going.

No pressure.

But the thought of having a quiet dinner with Lynsey Milton did appeal to him. He'd enjoyed meeting her and saving her from Lucy. He liked the conversation when they'd sat next to each other at lunch yesterday, even if the always-eager mayor and the other committee members had kept a close eye on both of them.

Tonight, when he showed her the house, they'd be alone with no nosy, well-meaning chaperones watching them as if they were still in another century. Good food, interesting discussions, getting to know each other. What could go wrong?

This could go wrong in, oh, so many ways, Lynsey decided after changing her clothes twice. It had grown colder outside, not unusual for the Panhandle, but certainly not the balmy warmth of temperatures in the sixties or seventies that could also occur here even in the winter. Since the sun went down earlier due to Daylight Savings Time changing each fall, it would be close to full dark by the time she made her way up the street to the Townsend house—known as

Magnolia Manor. She hoped she hadn't been too presumptuous when she'd asked Jon to show her his home. She wanted to see it for research purposes and so she could become more intimate with the founding family's history. What if he resented her being so nosy, or thought she only wanted to snoop?

Or course, she was being nosy and did want to snoop so too late to change that tactic. She really did want to get to know him better, too.

Yet, he was here to work with the town, not flirt with the committee chairman. But she was looking forward to seeing him again. He was a nice, easy-going man who appeared a bit conflicted about the progress of this town. Not someone she had to instantly get to know. She'd given up on relationships since her job demanded a lot of travel and weeks away from home.

Too late to back out now. She was already running late.

Finally deciding on jeans, boots and a maroon tunic sweater, she grabbed her phone and shoved it into a leather wristlet along with her room key, some cash and her lipstick. Then she put on her black wool coat and started the short trek up Lake Street to Magnolia Manor. She loved the sidewalks all around the lake. The walkway that followed the street had history markers placed in front of most of the elegant Victorian and Queen Anne estates and some of the smaller cottages, too. Even the tiny library held historical significance as being the oldest and smallest library in the state of Florida.

The paved path around the lake also allowed for views of the stunning homes across the water. Walking the circle had provided her with exercise and lots of ideas.

However, when she reached the front entry to Magnolia Manor and looked up at the turret room on the third floor, Lynsey's heart stopped. With the sun setting in the west, a soft shimmer of light fell across the massive white house, coloring it with a creamy brightness that made it look like a giant wedding cake all aglow with candlelight. Two giant magnolia trees stood sentinel on both sides of the house, their waxy leaves shooting up to the sky. They would be stunning when they bloomed in the spring.

The scene took her breath away.

Lynsey swallowed back the emotions flooding over her, the cold of dusk seeping into her bones as she remembered why she'd become involved in restoring historical towns to their former beauty. This had become a personal quest for her, but she didn't talk much in her presentations about the house that had once been a big part of her life.

She couldn't bring back the past but she wanted to move the past into the future, keeping in mind she needed to respect it and never forget it. This town wasn't just quaint and old-fashioned. It had started out in the 1880s as a forward-thinking resort community that recognized the arts and education, as well as diverse spirituality and recreation. A rare mission in those days. One that had survived and thrived for decades, evident in the beautiful white Springlake Assembly building down the way where the townspeople still held assembly meetings as well as a festival which celebrated their faith and the four cornerstones on which the town had been built.

Springlake could still promote the Springlake Festival and more if she managed to make the townspeople see her vision. Shaking her head, she moved up the walkway and stepped up onto to the long porch that some would call a veranda. She could imagine sitting in one of the white rocking chairs with a cup of tea.

Then she wondered why Jon lived alone. She'd heard so much about him, she felt as if she knew him better now. According to the mayor, he was a bachelor, much to the dismay of many of the single women in town.

"They've all tried to ply him with food and flirting and invitations to parties and family gatherings. Sometimes he accepts and sometimes he politely declines. Every mother in town wants Jon Townsend to be her son-in-law, for so many reasons."

Lynsey could imagine those reasons. He was attractive and shy, adorable really. He was single and certainly eligible. Not to mention, he lived in a historic Victorian mansion and probably had a portfolio worth millions. The man had a lot of assets.

She only thought about how he'd grabbed her this morning and put himself between her and a mad goose. That memory would forever be etched in her heart.

She was about to knock on one of the intricate stained-glass doors but stopped to study the magnolia blossoms and shimmering greenery of what had to be a Tiffany design in the half-glass inserts. Before she could put her numb hand against the glass, the door opened and there he stood.

"Oh, hi," she said, brushing at her hair. "I was admiring the stained-glass inlay. Tiffany? Are these doors original to the house?"

"Hello to you, too," he replied, laughing. "They are Tiffany and, yes, they are original to the house. We've tried to keep the character throughout the years. And the big magnolias on each side of the yard have been here for over a century. They've survived storms and blight and anything else Mother Nature has thrown at them. The trees and garden have been pampered and cared for by the Garden Club. Come in and I'll tell you all about it."

Lynsey rarely got nervous around people. Now she felt as tongue-tied as a schoolgirl crushing on a football player as she entered the house and stood staring up at him. He'd probably *been* a football player. "Thank you. It's chilly."

"So I noticed. I made a fire in the den fireplace."

Lynsey stopped at the wide mahogany staircase. "This is beautiful. I love the intricate carvings on the newel posts and the detailing on the stair spindles. And that circular first landing is very interesting."

Did she sound as goofy as she felt? She couldn't help

herself. This was a real treat. "I'm sorry. I don't normally gush but…I do love historic houses."

He waited, probably so she'd explain that comment, but she just smiled and kept her hand on a stair spindle.

"We've had to replace a few stair parts over the years," he said, touching one of the heavy rounded newel posts. "I ran up and down these stairs many times growing up. Come to think of it, I still run up and down them at times since I seem to always be late for something."

He escorted her past the formal dining room, stopping to let her admire the long table and set of eight matching chairs centered over what looked like an original Aubusson carpet. She noticed the many family portraits in both the dining room and the formal living room on the other side, which held more antique furnishings and high-backed sofas and settees.

Noticing one distinct face, she looked at Jon and then back to the painting. "Wow, the resemblance is uncanny."

Jon looked confused then followed her gaze. "Oh, that's my grandfather." Then he pointed to a smaller portrait off to the side. "That's my dad. He never wanted to do a portrait so I took a photo and enlarged it."

Lynsey studied the candid photo of an older man in a boat out on the lake, holding a big fish. "You look like him, too," she said. "Mayor Barton told me he died about five years ago. I'm so sorry about…both your parents."

"He was a good man but sometimes hard to deal with," Jon said, his bright eyes going dark for a moment. "He and my mother were so in love. I don't think either of us ever quite got over her death."

Then he ran a hand over his hair. "Sorry." He lifted a hand to encompass the sunny living room that had once been called a parlor. "We serve tea at four every afternoon."

She grinned, realizing he was teasing her. "With tiny scones, petit fours, and cucumber sandwiches?"

"If you insist."

She laughed. "I'm trying to imagine you sipping hot tea."

"I've been known to indulge in a little Earl Grey," he said on a hint of promise and with a twinkle in his eyes. "Let me take your coat. I only have coffee and water tonight."

"Coffee sounds good," she said, thinking she'd probably had enough but the fire and coffee would warm her. She took off her coat and he laid it and her purse on the bench of a chunky hall tree that looked like it had been carved from walnut.

The den was cozy, just a small room off the massive kitchen that had probably once been a maid's chambers. The paneled walls spoke of another era while the many plaques and framed awards on the focal wall told of a well-respected family's life. The furniture included a worn burgundy leather couch with soft cushions and a white throw, next to a checkered side chair that looked comfortable. One wall held several varieties of books.

"The house has been updated through the years," he explained when he brought in the coffee on a tray with some crackers and cheese. "My assistant insisted I provide appetizers," he said on a laugh. "Oh and, by the way, she left dinner. She makes a wonderful Italian casserole. It's like lasagna but with ziti noodles. There's plenty for two."

Lynsey pivoted and gave him a surprised look. "Are you asking me to stay for dinner, Jon?"

"I think I am," he replied. "If you'd like."

She would like but should she accept? Why did this man make her long for romantic dinners by the fire?

"If you have other plans…"

"No, nothing except going over reports and creating charts."

"To impress all of us?"

"Yes, of course." She relaxed and nodded. She had to eat and she needed to hear more about the history of this house. "I like Italian food."

"Then it's settled. After the tour, you and I will sit down and have a good meal. And get to know each other a little better."

This meeting could turn out to be better than any meeting in a conference room. She'd be able to ask Jon questions and gain a new perspective on the town his ancestors had created. And maybe a new perspective on this man, too.

"Okay."

He looked both relieved and unsure. "That's settled. Where would you like to start the tour?"

After they'd nibbled some cheese and sipped their drinks, Lynsey followed him out into the hallway and stared at the sun's waning rays settling over the lake and trees. "How about at the beginning?"

He laughed at that. "This could take all night."

Lynsey laughed, too. She needed to work but something told her this would be much better than studying charts and making projections. She usually learned the good stuff from chatting with people who knew the history of a town. And who better to know the history than the handsome guy living in Magnolia Manor?

Chapter Four

"Thank you for the tour, Jon," Lynsey said at dinner.

The house went beyond her expectations. A classic gothic Victorian scented with lemon wax and potpourri and just a hint of mustiness that spoke of both the past and the future. Jon entertained her with a story for each room, his explanations animated and endearing, the images of elegant ladies and handsome gentleman strolling through the house and laughing down by the lake coming alive in her mind. He was a true Southern gentleman.

They'd taken their plates out to the sunroom—or conservatory as it had been called when the house was first built.

"That's a fancy word," Jon had told her as they filled their plates. "We call it the sunroom now and ... it's heated and cooled in the summer. This old place gets drafty year-round, however."

Lynsey sat down and glanced from one side of the long-enclosed room to the other. It extended on each side of the house and led to another smaller open porch on one side, so she had a view of the stately trees and glowing streetlights on Lake Drive and a perfect view of the lake down below the back yard. She took in the parlor ferns and potted palm trees gracing the corners and the wicker furniture centered near seaside paintings. The glass-encased room was elegant and peaceful with shell-shaped wall sconces providing muted creamy lamplight. The lights shining from the garden and the houses across the lake gave the whole view a romantic feel. They sat in one corner where a small Victorian-style wrought iron bistro table held a flickering candle poured in a ceramic bowl in the shape of a scallop shell.

"You get this view every night," she said, the statement whispered.

"Every night in every season and from every corner," he replied, his words husky and hushed. "Funny how it never goes away and it never gets old."

She made a wry face. "I can't help it. I'm awestruck."

He stared across the table at her. "Me, too."

Glad he couldn't see her blushing, Lynsey shook her head. "You know this isn't a date, right?"

He drew back in shock, his hand going to his heart. "Wow, that's the most direct brush-off I've ever heard."

Lynsey's skin went hot. "No, that's not a brush-off. I didn't mean to imply anything. It's just that we'll be working together a lot over the next few months, I hope."

"You hope? So you do like me?"

He was messing with her head. "Yes, I like you. You're a great tour guide and I'm having an intimate home-cooked dinner overlooking the lake. It could be so easy, forgetting my place. I'm here for a purpose, an important assignment."

"Your place? An assignment? Are you saying I'm too good for you? Or that you're too good for me?"

"Stop doing that," she said, slapping at his arm with a gentle rebuttal. "I'm saying things could get awkward. My boss back in Atlanta wants me to make this work and … it's a big challenge. Especially when you're being so nice and looking at me like that."

"Relax," he finally said, his keen eyes on her. "I shouldn't be flirting with you. That can lead to all kinds of issues."

Hiding her disappointment, Lynsey nodded and took a long sip of water. She did feel the warmth that flowed so easily between them and she had noticed his flirting. Reminding herself of what was at stake, she said, "Exactly. Conflict of interest, fraternizing, you name it."

"Fraternizing? That's a term I haven't heard in years."

"People will talk."

"Well, we can't risk that. I mean, we only just met yesterday and what with Lucy still out roaming the lake and pouting, we simply have to ignore the food, candlelight, and the view. Not to mention, we've been set up by some master planners who obviously couldn't resist another bit of meddling in my love live, and yet we have to agree we can only be friends and business acquaintances."

"Exactly. Thank you for understanding." Thinking she should be relieved, Lynsey only felt deflated. If she'd met Jon Townsend under different conditions, she might be more inclined to see where this could go. But no. Too soon and too much was at stake, including her career. Especially her career.

"Let's have cookies by the fire," he suggested once they were done with the salad and casserole. "Unless you've had enough of me?"

"I'd like a cookie," she replied. "I can't get over this house. All these rooms with nooks and crannies, so many elegant bedrooms and bathrooms."

"Added through the years, thankfully." He shrugged. "And I didn't even take you to the turret room." Giving her a raised eyebrow glance, he whispered, "I'd never do that on our first date even though this isn't officially a first date."

She mock-glared at him. "Why? Too many secrets hidden away?"

He shot her a mysterious grin before taking their plates to the kitchen. "I'll never tell." Then he added. "It's better to go up there in daylight. My father always said that was Grandfather's office and the grandfather before him and so on and so on. It was my dad's office for many years."

She helped him clean the plates and put away the leftovers. Then he pulled out cocoa, sugar and milk, and started making hot chocolate on the six-burner gas stove.

Watching him measure and stir while he made rich hot cocoa did something to Lynsey's soul that felt a lot like butterflies lifting through her system. But she tamped that feeling down.

"Why isn't your office up in the turret?" she asked, remembering the big upstairs room across from the massive master bedroom that he used as an office. It had a great view of the lake and the old gazebo she'd spotted this morning. But it was messy and cozy and his alone. Which made him even more endearing and down-to-earth.

The turret room must have been special to his ancestors. Why not him?

He finished heating the hot chocolate and poured it into two mugs then threw in some miniature marshmallows. "Because it's stuffed with old documents and newspapers and well … I'm not sure what else. Ethel keeps telling me we need to go through it and see what's important and what's not."

"Oh, I'm with Ethel on that," Lynsey said, taking the mug he offered her. "I love nothing more than reading through old documents and letters."

Jon brought a plate of cookies over to the den and offered her one before he set it on the chunky coffee table. "Well, you'd have a field day. A lot of history is buried in that big round room, but I can't seem to make myself go through it. Maybe because I've lost both my parents and I don't want to go down memory lane."

Lynsey's heart filled with sympathy for him. "I'm sorry. That must have been so tough on you." She hadn't pushed him when he'd mentioned his parents earlier. Now she could see the pain and grief in his eyes. "Would it make things better if I helped you?"

He sipped his drink and broke off a piece of oatmeal cookie, his gaze squarely on her. "I think anything I undertake would be better if you're involved."

She accepted that something was brewing between them but she'd have to be very careful not to encourage him too much. Yet she couldn't refuse him. He seemed lonely here in this creaky, rambling house. "I'd be honored," she said before she dove into her own chocolate-chip-pecan cookie. Stress eating had always been her downfall.

"Then we'll set a time ... maybe one weekend? How long do you plan to stay?"

Lynsey put down her hot chocolate and smiled at him. "That depends on a lot of things," she said. "If I can't win everyone over to my plan for downtown Springlake, then I'll be called back to Atlanta pronto." And probably fired.

"We can't allow that," he said with a frown. "At least stay until you help me clear out that turret. I'm afraid of spiders, you understand."

She laughed out loud at that. "Right."

Jon sure did make her laugh a lot. And that scared her more than any old spider ever could.

Two days later, Jon entered the post office to mail some documents and saw Paul Caldwell behind the counter. Paul ruled the roost at the local post office and knew everything about everybody in town. Jon braced himself for what Paul might have to say.

"Good morning, Jon," Paul called, his gray ponytail neat and tidy. He wore a Mack McAnally T-shirt that showed his good taste in music, at least. "How's the law?"

"Still the law," Jon replied, as he always did. "Busy as always what with births, and deaths, and land transactions."

Paul took Jon's envelopes. "I heard you had a visitor the

other night."

"Yeah, a few squirrels played on the roof."

"You know what I mean. I've seen that fancy uptown development lady strolling around with phone attached to her ear. She seems to know her stuff."

Jon waited a beat, knowing more was coming.

Paul handled the documents and gave him his receipt. "Is she gonna mess with our town?"

"That's her job," Jon replied. "She has some good ideas for changes that could bring us into the future. Things such as a performing art center, art galleries, and upscale retail shops."

"I like the past," Paul said. "And I sure don't do upscale."

"Lynsey likes the past, too. She works hard to incorporate the past with the future."

"Why mess with a good thing?"

Jon looked at Paul and smiled. "Why not expand on a good thing?"

"So she won you over?"

"I'm considering all angles," Jon said. "And I have to get back to work."

Paul nodded then chuckled. "You know I'm just an old hippie. I go with the flow."

"Then you will continue to fit right in," Jon replied. "I'll see you on the next go-round."

He walked out into the crisp, cold wind and wondered if the whole town thought he'd lost his senses just because he'd had an intimate dinner with a newcomer. All around him, the streets were beginning to shine with Christmas lights and bright red and green decorations. A dolphin-shaped yard display would dazzle in bright blue when they officially held the Christmas festival. The three jumping dolphins wore bright red-light scarfs. Palm trees and oversized seashells would complete the scene.

And somewhere along the route, Santa would be carried

into the sky by alligators dressed in the University of Florida Gators' colors of bright orange and blue, mixed with the Florida State colors of garnet and gold. That had transpired after a heated town hall meeting years ago.

Christmas in Florida, always a paradox.

Jon loved this little town even if he'd resented moving back.

The attractive, smart newcomer wanted to change his town and his world. He might have defended her to ornery Paul. What was everyone else thinking or saying?

And why did he care?

Lynsey was a refreshing change in a world that liked routine. A lot of hard-working people around here who liked the slow pace of living in paradise and knowing their neighbors, the pace of attending church on Sunday and going to work at the same jobs on Monday. Would it hurt to shake that up a bit with a makeover? Or would the essence of Springlake be gone forever?

Well, his ancestors and the entourage that had followed them had certainly changed things when they'd decided to build a resort and retreat. Their forward-thinking methods could still be applied today. The love of art, faith, nature, and progressiveness still could apply. Especially with the sad downtown area of Springlake.

Is that what you would want, Grandfather?

Maybe it was time to shake up his world and embrace the needed changes that could make this diamond in the rough shine again.

Might do him good since he'd enjoyed listening to Lynsey's ideas at the meeting and her hopes for Springlake. What if he had other motives? What if he had let her influence him too much? It had been a while since Jon had been so intrigued by a woman. He'd enjoyed showing off his home to her and her enthusiasm was contagious. She'd made him realize how alone he was, sitting up on the hill over the lake.

Deciding to take the long walk home, Jon managed to avoid any further questions about where his loyalties lay. Soon he came up on Magnolia Manor, but instead of going inside he strolled down to the old gazebo. He really needed to have it repaired. It would look pretty all lit up and decorated for the holidays.

That brought back memories of when his mother and her friends would go all out on decorating for Christmas. The gazebo would be festive with red bows and all kinds of greenery and lights. Then the kids would gather for s'mores and hot chocolate and sing Christmas carols. Jon missed those times now, but when he was growing up he sometimes thought the whole process was overkill.

Overkill? He'd been sullen and stupid and spoiled by all of this. Now, he only wanted to protect this old place.

When he strolled around the huge live oak that blocked most of the gazebo, he saw a woman standing inside the octagon-shaped structure, staring out at the lake.

Lynsey.

Did the fates have something in mind for him since he kept running into her?

No, because it was easy to see anyone on any given day along the lake.

Jon decided he'd explore that fate theory, or as his mother used to call these type moments—faith theories—so he walked down to the gazebo and stood to the side. "What do you see out there?"

She whirled, her eyes widening, her smile warming his heart. "Hello. I was just thinking about you."

Jon accepted that he was attracted to Lynsey. But he couldn't let her or anyone else know that right now. The future of his home depended on how he handled this new development.

"Funny, I was thinking about you, too." He moved down the slope to the gazebo. "Any sign of Lucy?"

"She took her brood to the other side of the lake,"

Lynsey said, questions in her eyes. "She doesn't like me. Why were you thinking about me?"

"I don't know," he admitted. "People are talking. Some want changes and some will resist till the day they're buried in the town cemetery and probably beyond that."

Lowering her head, she shivered as a gust of wind swept off the water. "I'm the reason for the buzz?"

"You, and the fact that we had dinner together the other night. Scandalous, I know. That's part of being in a small town. Everyone knows your business and sometimes they forget we're well past the turn of the century."

Her frown softened. "We didn't do anything inappropriate, and besides your assistant practically forced us together, not that I'm blaming her. I could have declined but I wanted to talk to you. It makes sense the head of the restoration committee and the person who's in charge of creating the restoration plan will have to meet several times."

He glanced out over the water and saw the ducks and geese gliding like ice skaters across the way. So she'd had her own motives last night. What if people did see this as a conflict of interest? "Yes, I agree, maybe in public with other people next time."

She looked perplexed and then her lips went down, regret surrounding her. "I understand." Then she started gathering her tote bag. "I'd like to think we're not quiet that old-fashioned but I don't want anything that looks inappropriate to cause you trouble."

Jon realized he'd made a big mistake. She thought he was embarrassed. "No. I didn't mean that the way it sounds."

Looking relieved, she said, "Good, because I do want to talk to you so I'm glad you stopped here. This gazebo represents everything that's wonderful about Springlake. I've heard comments that it needs to be torn down. Some want to refurbish it and make it shine as the centerpiece of the lake again. Frankly, I can't understand why it's been neglected."

"That's my fault," he said. "Technically, it's on my property and I keep promising to restore it, but I get busy or bury my head in a law book and things don't get done in a timely fashion."

"This is a special place. I knew that the day I saw it. I can see the beauty underneath the old jasmine vines and the weathered wood."

Impressed, Jon nodded. "It's still there, yes."

Lynsey turned back to one of the sturdy posts holding up the gazebo. "Have you ever noticed the initials carved on this post?"

Jon's gaze followed the direction of her pointing finger. "Where?"

She peeled back a thick jasmine vine and put her hand on the etched wood.

He looked at the carved initials and then looked at her. "I haven't thought about this in years. JT and LM."

"Carved inside a heart," she replied. "Notice anything else about these initials, Jon?"

He stared again. "They were carved by my great-great-great-grandfather and the woman who became his wife."

"That might be true," she said. Then she smiled. "We have the same initials."

Jon looked at the carving again and then stared at her. "You're right. I didn't put that together. JT and LM. How about that?"

"We need to restore this gazebo," she said, her gaze wandering out over the water and then back to him. "Please keep the carved initials." With a smile and a sigh, she went on. "Their story can be the focus of bringing the town back to life—but also bringing it up to speed and modern."

"I remember they met around 1910, right before Christmas." He stared up at the house. "The whole story is buried somewhere in the files and papers in the turret room."

Lynsey almost clapped her hands, but refrained. Which

made him want to laugh. "We have to start digging."

"Let's see if anyone else notices before we point this out to them," he said on a conspiring whisper. "And you know what, let's not worry about what everyone is thinking or saying. We both want the same thing, right?"

"Yes, we want Springlake to be the best it can be. And so do they," she said, her hand touching the carving. "This is a good thing, Jon."

Jon realized fate was in his favor today, after all. And maybe God had sent him the one person who could get him out of his self-imposed stupor. "I think you're right."

She sensed his hesitation. "Only you don't seem so sure."

"I'm contemplating. This old thing shouldn't be that hard to restore, right?"

"No. A few volunteers and some new paint, sturdy beams and then we decorate it. Really, an easy way to get people's attention and involvement." She started pacing, something she seemed to do a lot. "Meantime, you and I have to get into that room and find out about your ancestors. What a romantic story. What's better than a Christmas romance?"

"Nothing," he said, wanting to hug her for being so enthusiastic. Watching her would have to be enough for now. "Right now, I think a Christmas romance might bring this whole town together."

She shot him a smile that made him think of cuddling by a fire with hot chocolate. "It's the perfect idea."

"So you can convince all of us to change Springlake for the better?"

"Yes. Isn't that what you want?"

The panic in her eyes made him realize she'd been focusing on the work, not the moment. "Of course."

She put a hand on his arm. "I'm glad I ran into you."

He grinned back at her, hoping he looked convinced and convincing. "I'm glad I took the long way home." At least that much was true.

"So let's bring this up at the next meeting. If we start small and you allow me to be involved in this one project, I can win over some of the last holdouts. Then we can hold an open house, maybe in the Assembly Building, to show them the completed plans. I don't want to destroy the historical aspects of Springlake. I want people can appreciate this town for what it is—a good place to call home."

She touched her fingers to the initials again. "This is an amazing Christmas surprise."

"A complete surprise," he admitted. *She* was a surprise. "I remember my mother telling the story of how that Jonathon and his Lettie met right here before the gazebo had even been built. Grandmother Lettie is the reason it got built."

"I can't wait to find out more about her."

He could easily imagine walking home to see Lynsey every day. He'd have to tamp down those thoughts until they had a master plan that worked for the good of the town and, somehow, he had to figure out why he kept dragging his feet on things.

But he'd keep the image of her standing with her hand touching that carved heart in his daydreams and enjoy it for a long time to come.

Chapter Five

"I can't move up the timeline, Richard. Christmas is just around the corner and everyone is busy. I need *more* time. I can't pressure these people."

Lynsey sank down on the desk chair in the guest room at the hotel, her nerves shivering as a chilly rain poured outside the double-windows. She'd met so many citizens who were ready for a more modern town. A lot of them had volunteered to help renovate the gazebo. "I have a project going that I think will soften the die-hards."

"What kind of project?" Richard Whitlow asked, his Atlanta drawl indicating he didn't believe her. "The project is to bring the town into the twenty-first century, remember? You're the project manager and I've got board members to report back to, so this had better be good."

"Working on that, one building and one person at a time," Lynsey said. Then she told him about the gazebo. "I'm about to meet with several members from the Christmas Festival Committee, mostly Garden Club members who carry a lot of clout. The gazebo work has already started and if I can convince Jon Townsend to let us decorate Magnolia Manor, people will see that even he's in on this revitalization."

Richard let out a sound that could have been a happy laugh or a miserable groan. "Did you say Jon Townsend, as in the Townsends, as in the man who actually started Springlake, Florida?"

Thinking she'd gained points, Lynsey rushed ahead. "Yes. He's a sixth-generation Townsend with the same name, and the head of the restoration committee. He's slowly coming around on this whole revitalization and cityscape plan." Deciding to give Richard one more tidbit, she added, "He's in on the gazebo renovation, but I think Magnolia Manor, the family home, needs to be part of the festivities."

"You have till Christmas," Richard barked. Lynsey was pretty sure it had been a happy bark. "Then we'll get started early next year."

"I won't let you down, I promise," she told her boss.

Lynsey loved her work so she wasn't too worried about lingering. Richard was just a grumbling teddy bear who also believed in saving as much of America's past as they could. But they did serve under a board of directors that volunteered their time and also a lot of their money.

Working for a non-profit meant she had a good job and salary but that couldn't stop her from being fired is she wasted anybody's time or money. She didn't want that to happen. She'd worked too hard to become a project manager and hoped to be a regional manager one day.

Three weeks until Christmas. Could she convince Jon to break his no-decorations policy at Magnolia Manor?

Technically, he hadn't been as excited about renovating the gazebo as she had implied. She still had to ask him about decorating the house, too. Ethel had told her a lot when she's run into the jovial older woman at the Side Street Café. After introducing herself and sitting down to chat, Ethel had explained to Lynsey that he didn't decorate much since he usually went out of town during the holidays.

"Skiing or off to some warmer part of Florida. He meets up with friends and tries to hide his pain and grief."

Would he be willing to stay home this Christmas?

Would that help Jon to not be so lonely? She'd do her part to make his holidays special and keep him involved.

That would mean a lot of time with him. Could she handle that?

She had to. Richard would want updates.

What she'd told Richard was just a tiny exaggeration. Jon would come around. He had to even if he didn't seem that excited about her coming here to interrupt his staid routines. They did have plans to tackle the turret room. What would they find?

Regaining her energy, Lynsey did what she did best. She made notes and prepared to face the Garden Club members this afternoon and talk about her plans. That should be easy enough.

"They will smile very sweetly and then cut you like a deadhead on a plant."

Lynsey did a careful sweep of the roomful of prim women wearing pearls and holding to their purses like Queen Elizabeth. They'd begun filing into the small meeting room inside the assembly building one by one, all in colorful fall and winter suits. Even though the rain had stopped, the sky was still dark. She watched as the women placed their umbrellas on a table in the back. Prepared. She hoped she was, too.

"They look docile enough to me. Almost pleasant."

Amy Corez, whom Lynsey had met two days ago when she'd attended church at the quaint white chapel that was almost as old as the town, rolled her brown eyes and laughed out loud. "You've got a lot to learn, City Girl."

"Then teach me," Lynsey said. "I don't want to upset the very people I need to help me pull this off."

Amy tossed her short black curls and motioned Lynsey

to put her tote down on a chair in front. Then she took Lynsey by the arm and marched her toward the kitchen. "I joined about four years ago because I love gardening and I wanted to contribute to the beautification of the town." She said those last four words while doing air-quotes with her fingers. "I'm an Air Force wife and my husband goes on long missions. I needed something to fill the time while my kids are in school."

"Okay, so how did it go?" Lynsey asked, almost afraid to know.

Amy busied herself with pouring coffee and putting out cookies and fruit. "At first, not so well. I can be sassy or so I'm told."

Lynsey smiled at that. She liked Amy even if her new friend was an avid Alabama football fanatic. They had connected since they were so close in age. Plus, Amy knew things. The more information Lynsey could take in, the more prepared she'd be at the next meeting. "I can't imagine you upsetting these upstanding citizens."

"I called a camellia a rose," Amy admitted, her dark eyebrows winging up. "I thought for sure we'd have to get out the smelling salts."

They both giggled at that.

Then Lynsey heard a definite clearing of a throat behind them.

Amy whirled. "Oh, Mrs. Montgomery, we didn't hear you come in."

"So I see." The woman stared at them with a sour frown, her grayish-white hair perfectly stiff and curled. "I'd like my coffee with cream, please, Amy."

"We've got everything ready," Amy said, turning to finish up her task. "Have you met Lynsey Milton, our project manager for the downtown restoration?"

"No," the woman said. Staying by the kitchen door she looked at Lynsey with what might have registered as a slight smile. "But I've heard so much I decided to come in here and see what all the fuss is about. Nonsense, this rebuilding the entire town!"

Amy let out a soft sigh. "Lynsey Milton, this is Virginia Montgomery, a descendant of one of the founding fathers of Springlake and the president of the Garden Club."

Lynsey extended her hand. "Hello, Mrs. Montgomery. It's so nice to meet you."

Virginia Montgomery shook her hand and stared her in the eye. "I didn't make it to the first meeting regarding this revitalization. I'm interested in hearing why you need the Garden Club's help."

Lynsey straightened her spine. "I want to talk to the members about helping to renovate the gazebo and possibly decorating Magnolia Manor—maybe for an open house."

Virginia lifted her chin and held up her nose. "Jon Townsend will never go for that."

"I'll explain in the meeting," Lynsey said, looking at her watch. "Which is due to start soon."

"I know what time it starts," Virginia said. "I have the gavel in my purse."

With that, she swirled in a puff of too-sweet perfume and headed for the podium at the front of the now-full room of women and a few brave men.

"I think that conversation went about as well as can be expected," Amy said after Virginia had left the kitchen. "Now go out there and show 'em your stuff. And don't show fear. They can smell that like they sniff gardenias. And if any one of them says, "Well, bless your heart, be prepared for what comes next."

Lynsey laughed. "I know that old trick. I did grow up in Atlanta, after all. I cut my teeth on reading good Southern fiction and I have three aunts who taught me a lot about southern charm and cattiness."

"You got this, girl," Amy said. "I'll take out the treats. This is gonna be good."

Lynsey had handled tough audiences before but she had

to admit, when she entered the room and sat down up front and waited for Virginia Montgomery to introduce her, her heart hammered like a woodpecker hitting a cypress tree.

What had she gotten herself into now?

"What a delightful idea."

"So impressed with your presentation, Miss Milton. Are you related to the Florida Miltons? You know, the county seat up on the Blackwater River."

"No, ma'am," she said, smiling. "I'm familiar with Milton. A lovely town."

"No better than ours," someone else said. "That gazebo needs to be renovated. I might not agree with this whole plan, but what can it hurt to bring the gazebo back to life. And such a sweet, romantic thing to do for Christmas, telling the story of the initials on the post."

Virginia Montgomery came forward, her expression as tick-tight as her fingers clutching her sensible purse. "You have some innovative ideas, Miss Milton. I might have to drag out all of my Christmas decorations." Her expression might have held a fleeting smile. "I remember the gazebo back in the day. Many a marriage proposal took place in that little structure. I have to tip my hat to you. You somehow got Jon Townsend to agree to let us renovate it, and that's saying something."

After Virginia nodded and turned to walk away, Lynsey turned to Amy and they did a high-five, both silently screaming in awe. "Wow," Amy said. "Just wow."

The receiving line ended and most of the older ladies left with their umbrellas open to the mist while others stayed to help clean up.

Amy's grin said it all. "We did it. I mean, you did it. I just passed out cookies."

"You gave me some good pointers," Lynsey whispered as people kept coming up to her to shake her hand and offer to help. "Do you think we really won over Mrs. Montgomery? Or was she just being polite with her parting comments?"

Amy took the empty plates Lynsey handed her. "Well, she didn't melt or turn to dust, so there is that." After putting the plates in the sink full of soapy water, she turned to Lynsey. "I'd say you won her over. That woman is never polite to anyone."

"I caught her smiling during my PowerPoint," Lynsey said before she guzzled half a glass of water. "I've never been so nervous."

"You had them at romance," Amy replied, her eyes bright and her dimples big. "A lot of them have lost their husbands and many of those husbands were war veterans. They remember the good ol' days and … I think they remember romance, in spite of their curmudgeonly attitudes."

Lynsey couldn't argue with that. "That's good to consider. I can't imagine losing a husband, in war or in life."

"I worry about mine," Amy said. "He loves his work and we do have several military bases nearby—Eglin and Hurlburt are Air Force and cover a lot of the coastal territory, plus we have the Naval Station in Pensacola, too. The Blue Angels put on a good show every year and we all support them."

"I'm adding those factors to the whole picture," Lynsey said. "More romance and more heroes. More reasons to live in Springlake since it's located only an hour or so from the Gulf."

"What about Jon?" Amy asked, her tone low.

Surprised and wary, Lynsey glanced around. "You mean Jon Townsend?"

"What other Jon would I mean? Small town, big ears. Are you two an item?"

Lynsey shook her head a little too fast. "No, no. We're working on this project together. He's the head of the planning committee. We're just friends."

Amy held her arm. "Okay, okay. All good reasons to be seen around town together. Personally, I'm happy for both of you. Mercy, even I've tried to set the man up but he's kind of stubborn. A bachelor and I mean with a capital B."

"He's a nice guy though, and yes, he's probably lonely, I think he'd prefer to meet someone on his own, without so much interference or influence."

"He likes you," Amy insisted. "Everyone can see that." Then she winked. "Now that's romance, girl."

"There's no romance between Jon and me," Lynsey replied. Although having that intimate dinner with him had shouted romance.

"Keep telling yourself that," Amy countered. "Jon doesn't know it yet, either."

Lynsey wanted to be irritated but she couldn't deny she liked Jon and she didn't want to alienate her new friend. "Let's move on to other subjects."

"Let's." Amy gave her an understanding smile. "I've overstepped, something I'm kinda good at."

"No, you haven't," Lynsey said as she gathered her things. "I do like Jon only I have a job to do and he has to uphold the Townsend reputation."

"Can't those two things coexist?" Amy asked as other women walked by carrying coffee cups and the leftover cookies. "You didn't come here to ruin him. You came to make this town even more special than it already is."

"I hope so," Lynsey said. "I have a lot to get done in a small amount of time."

Amy picked up forks and napkins, her cap-sleeved floral blouse fluttering around her. "Then use every moment of that time wisely," she suggested. "Don't let a possibly good thing slip through your fingers."

Lynsey thanked Amy and then left the Springlake

Assembly building, too tired to admire the beautiful old place with a nice garden area by the lake. This had to be the toughest town revitalization she'd ever worked on and now, she only wanted her sweatpants and some soup in her room at the hotel. The weight of fighting off rumors and her own mixed feelings regarding Jon Townsend made her want to shed her business clothes and take a long jog around the lake. The rain that had started earlier only increased as a gray dusk settled over the trees and lake, so she hurried back to the hotel and put on her softest fleece leggings and matching hoodie. Stopping before she could order room service, Lynsey changed her mind. She needed fresh air, even if it was damp, rainy air. So she grabbed a raincoat and decided a good walk in the cold drizzle would help her to think straight. She talked to Got a lot on her long walks, and she prayed he'd listen.

Hoping the weather would improve tomorrow, she got excited about going up into the turret room with Jon later this week. What kind of secrets did Magnolia Manor hold?

And what kind of secrets did the man living there hold?

Jon watched the rain falling across the lake and wondered when he'd become so lonely. Ethel had left an hour ago. A pot of homemade vegetable-beef soup sat warm on the stove, fresh cornbread muffins nearby.

He should eat and then go back to his office to get some work done. Instead, he remembered sitting out in the sunroom with Lynsey. That had been a first, eating dinner in the sunroom.

His mother had allowed breakfast and sometimes snacks in the sunroom, but dinner was to be held in the formal dining room after his dad came down from his tower and joined them.

They'd had good discussions most nights. Other times, father and son would get into a heated argument.

"I want to go to FSU."

"You will attend Yale, following generations of Townsends."

"I have friends attending Florida State."

"You can see your friends on holidays and during the summer."

And so it had gone. Yale it was, only because Jon had lost his mother not long after that conversation and he'd do anything to make his father proud of him.

Turning away from the lake, he knew why he'd pushed people away. His father had been a good man, but a demanding one. His mother, gracious and kind to everyone. The light of his father's eyes. That light had gone out after her death.

Jon wasn't sure he could deal with that kind of pain. If love made a person go from happy and blessed to angry and numb, he wasn't sure he wanted to feel it. Marriage, children, loving someone—it was all too much. It had taken a toll on his father and that had made Jon's life lonely and uncertain. He had friends enough and his father made sure Jon and he were always on the pew at church each Sunday. No one ever knew how his father and he had suffered in silence at the end of the day.

Ethel Porter, a widow from an early age, had been one of his mother's best friends. She'd come to Jon's rescue after his mother died. She'd needed a job and Father had immediately hired her out of a sense of duty and because he was a benevolent man. But to Jon, she'd been an angel, like a Mary Poppins standing there at their door. His father gave her only one rule.

She should never disturb him when he was working.

Ethel and Jon adhered to that rule and left Jon Senior alone. Ethel would tend the house, buy the groceries and make sure Jon got off to school with everything he needed, and she also took Jon to church. She'd helped him with homework and science projects while his father stayed up in the turret rooms dealing with his financial holdings and practicing law. He'd leave to meet with clients or have clients come to their home and meet with him in a small conference room on the third floor that was now used for storage. Occasionally, and probably because Ethel had reminded him, Jonathon Senior would come down to admire a project or comment on a report card. His father had never been cruel, but he'd been indifferent.

Indifferent was the definition of pain, but his father had stayed that way to the bitter end.

Now Jon stood analyzing his feelings, still raw and bruised, and wondering why Lynsey Milton's presence had rocked his whole world and his self-determined vow to never fall in love. He could blame the changes that needed to come or he could be honest, at least to himself. He'd been shuddered and silent, moving around this big house like a lost knight searching for his kingdom. Searching for his princess. Searching for the kind of love that survived all things.

Lynsey would make a great princess because she could rule the world. And she could be the kind of woman to conquer all, even the heart of a lonely hunter.

Staring at his cell phone where he'd left it on the kitchen counter, Jon thought about calling her. No. He couldn't do that. So he grabbed a windbreaker and his old tennis shoes and made sure the stove was off. He'd have Ethel's soup later.

Right now, he could check on the progress down at the gazebo and take a long walk in the rain to clear his head. And maybe, pray about opening up his heart a little bit more.

Chapter Six

Lynsey left the hotel, taking a side door out, and turned toward Lake Street. The dark water drew her. She'd always loved being around water. It soothed her and calmed her down. She loved going to Lake Lanier, which was close to Atlanta, on her down time. Whenever she could, she'd drive the day-long trip from Atlanta to the Gulf Coast and spend a few days in a small beach cottage a friend owned.

Now as the rain turned to a mist and day turned to dark, she strolled the trail trying to imagine how these woods had looked back when Jonathon One had discovered the lake untamed and wild. What a sight this must have been, a perfectly round hole of water bubbling from a deep spring in the middle of a vast thicket. Soon after the town started developing, the Pensacola and Atlantic Railroad had charged its way through this wilderness, changing everything and opening up a whole world of commerce that stretched across the Florida Panhandle. While the line had changed names over the years and no longer carried passengers, it still existed even now. Lynsey loved the sound of the train coming through town.

She walked briskly in the damp, chilly air and took in the creamy lights from across the lake. Families settling in for the night. Homework to do and dinner to cook. Dad coming home to kiss his wife and children and let the dog out back. Life. This place teemed with life.

Springlake offered a different pace from the constant and endless traffic jams and never-ending construction in Atlanta, the crowds at any event, and the everyday push and pull of living in one of the South's most amazing cities.

Being in this small town made her calm and showed her how stressed she'd been. Her head down, Lynsey watched as rainwater splashed against her walking shoes.

I have to win this. I want to do this. I want to make a difference and create a positive outcome for all. Am I doing the right thing?

She looked up and ran right into the arms of Jon Townsend.

"Whoa," he said, reaching out to stop her from knocking him over. "You sure were deep in thought."

Lynsey's heart did a heavy bump as she tried to catch her breath. Seriously? The one person she needed to avoid? "I didn't see you coming." An understatement.

His arms still on hers, he looked her over. "You weren't watching ahead. What if Lucy had jumped out and squawked at you?"

She looked around, expecting the goose to grab her. "Doesn't she sleep?"

"She's probably huddled under some shrubs, yes."

Lynsey smiled at that. "But you're right. I wasn't watching where I was going. I was *thinking* ahead, however."

He stood back, his gaze moving over her face and hair. "Me, too. I needed some fresh air."

She shivered and pulled her raincoat tight. Whether from the cold mist or seeing him, she felt a chill coming on. "I thought I might clear my head but it's really cold."

He nodded and rubbed his hand down the sleeve of his windbreaker. "Yes, more than I realized. of one of my better ideas." Then he looked around. "Hey, Ethel left a pot of homemade soup and some corn muffins on the stove. Want to join me?"

Lynsey badly wanted some soup but she hesitated, trying to remember why she should avoid Jon. "I don't know. What about all those people who seem to be watching us? I think they hired Lucy as a spy."

"I thought we settled that," he reminded her. "I don't care what Lucy or anyone else might see, and I don't want you to worry. I'm a grown man. It's time I start acting like one."

Lynsey thought he looked like a grown man, even adorably wet right now, his hair plastered across his forehead in a way that enticed her fingers to fix it, and his eyes on her.

How could she refuse? "You're right. I normally don't let anyone intimidate me while I'm working. I take my job seriously and I work hard, and I don't mind reaching an agreeable compromise."

"A compromise? Wow, you just crushed any notions I had of another romantic dinner."

Telling her heart to behave, she stared up at him. "Were you planning a romantic dinner?"

"Not really." He looked out at the lights across the lake. "I just didn't want to eat alone. I came out to check on the gazebo. No work today, but the construction crew has strict orders to leave the initials alone. They plan to work around the carved heart."

Lynsey felt the arrow of that admission deep inside her heart. "That's good to hear." Then she said, "I didn't want to eat alone, either."

He held out his hand. "So let's you and I compromise. Let's forget about work for a couple of hours. Come to dinner, Lynsey."

She nodded and took his hand. His fingers entwined with hers made her feel safe and warm. A charge of awareness shot through her at lightning speed and sent a warning up to her brain.

THE CHRISTMAS GAZEBO

Be careful. Tread lightly. Stay on task. Pray.

Jon held her hand all the way back to his house but they didn't speak much. He glanced over at her, smiling. She smiled back, confusion warring with longing as hope and fear passed through her like a current going out to sea.

"We'll go in through the back," he said. "I'll hang our wet coats in the mudroom."

"Good," she said. "I'd hate to ruin that beautiful entryway." Or hear more gossip. If Jon wasn't worried, she shouldn't fret either.

"This house can't be ruined," he said. "Remember it's been standing for a long time and it's survived so many things."

"With a lot of memories holding it together."

"Yes. Now it needs new memories and I haven't been a good steward on that point. I've been hidden away more than I care to admit."

He gave her a glance that left her wanting to be a part of his new memories. Maybe she could bring up decorating his house for Christmas, but she didn't want to burst this fragile bubble with work suggestions. Maybe later they could talk about that.

Tonight, she just wanted soup and a warm spot to land, and she wouldn't mind holding Jon's hand for a while longer, either.

Jon warmed the hearty beef and vegetable soup and set the plate of crispy cornbread muffins on the counter. "You sure you want to eat in the kitchen?" he asked Lynsey after she'd taken a towel to her hair. Now she stood warming herself by the fire he'd immediately built after they came inside.

"Yes." She spun around, her hair falling in soft curls

around her sweatshirt. "I'm not exactly dressed for the formal dining room and … the sunroom is beautiful, but it's cozy near the fire."

"We can take our plates and bowls over," he suggested. "Since I'm going to be a grown-up now, I can do whatever I please, right?"

Lynsey giggled. "So you're really going rogue. We can eat sitting on the couch?"

"Yes. Another scandal."

"You're living on the edge, Jon."

"It feels good," he replied. "I might eat two cornbread muffins."

"If you bring the butter, I might do the same."

Soon they had trays on the coffee table and plates with bowls of steaming soup on their laps. He watched as Lynsey took a spoonful.

Lynsey closed her eyes. "Oh, this is so good. You can never fire Ethel."

Jon laughed. "Are you kidding? She's runs this place. I think her contract is iron-clad."

"Where does she live? Or is she like a fairy godmother that just appears?"

"She's human, but she lives down the lake in a little cottage that originally belonged to an interesting ancestor who was both an author and artist. In fact, the woman who originally owned the cottage was an aunt to our Loretta. Gertrude Ross—Aunt Gertie. A free-thinker from what I hear."

"Everyone here seems to be a free-thinker." Lynsey said. "Your Lettie sounds as if she had a strong spirit."

"She captured that Jonathon's heart," Jon said between bites of corn muffin. "Her Kodak camera is up in the attic somewhere."

Lynsey put down her spoon. "A treasure. We'll try to find it and clean it up. It should be in the museum—I mean, if you give permission."

Jon didn't hesitate. "I'd be glad to display it. I'm sure there's a lot of things that need to be in the museum."

"That can be a draw for bringing people to Springlake."

"We're not talking work, remember?"

Lynscy did a zip across her lips with her fingers. "I'm getting back to this soup."

They ate in silence for a while then Jon said, "It's nice to have someone to enjoy this good food."

Lynsey finished the last of her muffin and turned to face him. "Do you ever hold dinner parties or events in the house?"

Jon chuckled. "What do you think?"

"No?"

"Never occurred to me. Ethel holds book club meetings in the sunroom and the Garden Club has held their annual spring luncheon on the grounds, but I rarely invite anyone since I'm not the best at entertaining people."

"Do you go out to dinner?"

Jon leaned close. "Is that your way of asking me if I'm dating anyone, or are you just asking me out to dinner for our third date?"

"No." She pushed at her hair and then lifted her plate and put it on the tray. "Nothing like that. And this is not a date."

Jon couldn't resist teasing her. "Aren't you the least bit curious?"

"No. That is your business, but I haven't seen any signs to indicate you have a significant other," she said, recovering nicely. "I didn't get my hair torn out by a jealous woman at the Garden Club meeting earlier today. Of course, most of those women are old enough to be your grandmother." Before he could protest, she held up a finger. "And I have it on good authority that you are eligible and available so I don't have to ask you any trick questions. That's not my style."

Lawyer that he was, he wanted to question her. "Are you

glad I'm not exclusively dating someone?"

"As I said, it's none of my business."

"What about you?"

Her eyebrows lifted, her expression changing. "What do you mean?"

"Is there someone waiting for you back in Atlanta?"

"No," she said, looking down. "My parents have given up on that. I have two sisters who are married and settled. I'm the oldest, a classic overachiever, and the last holdout."

Jon got up to stoke the fire, thinking the fire in his heart was burning just fine. So she wasn't dating either. "We should have established all of this early on."

"We're not really dating," she pointed out, her argument sounding weak.

"Oh, no. But with all the rumors, I'd hate to surprise you with someone hidden in the attic."

"Is that why you don't go up to the turret room, Mr. Rochester?"

Confused, he said, "Excuse me?"

"The hero in the novel *Jane Eyre*?"

"Oh, him. Didn't he break Jane's heart?"

"He did. He was a bit of a confused cad. Jane mended her heart and came back to mend his, too."

He sat back down beside her. "Well, I don't have anyone hiding upstairs and I'm not a notorious heartbreaker." Then he quit teasing and admitted, "I'm rethinking my self-imposed bachelorhood since you came along."

"I think that's to be determined," she said, looking into his eyes in a way that told him he might be the brokenhearted one. "We seem to have different paths in life."

Jon touched a hand to her curls. "Well, we were on the same path tonight. I think our second date has been even better than the first one."

She got all twitchy and nervous. "We're not dating."

And he got serious again. "Then what are we doing?"

"We're two adults sharing time together over Ethel's amazing food."

He wanted to kiss her, but that would be a big mistake. So he smiled and dropped his hand. "I can make hot chocolate again."

"Hmm." She gave him a sweet grin. "With marshmallows?"

"Double marshmallows."

"Then I'm in."

Jon took that as a good sign. He moved to the kitchen, taking their empty soup bowls with him. Lynsey followed him and helped him tidy up.

The rain fell in soft sheets across the lawn, the backyard security light shining through the mist. "This storm isn't letting up," he said, thinking about their cozy fireside chat tonight. "I'm glad we ran into each other—literally."

"Me, too," she said, a new light shining in her eyes. "It's almost as if we were supposed to find each other out on that path."

"I agree," he said as he measured out cocoa powder and sugar then poured milk into the small pan. While he stirred, Lynsey found mugs and opened a fresh bag of marshmallows. She looked so at home.

"I needed that walk," she said. "Needed to think things through. I've never been in this situation before."

"What kind of situation?"

"One where I'm attracted to the head of the planning committee."

Jon stopped stirring and stared at her. "So you're admitting that?"

"Isn't it obvious?"

He watched the chocolate mix beginning to bubble and then turned down the heat to add a drop of vanilla. Moving closer, he reached for her. "I feel the same way and I know I've been obvious."

Her expression moved from wonder to

acknowledgement, her eyes widening and her smile softening. "Okay, so what do we do now?"

Jon threw caution to the wind and pulled her into his arms. "How about this?" He lowered his lips to hers and kissed her, a sweet touch of his mouth to hers.

Lynsey didn't push him away. Instead, she sighed and leaned into the kiss, held onto him, and turned it from an exploration to a definite destination.

A destination that felt like home.

Then she pulled away. "Jon?"

"Hmm?"

"I think the hot chocolate is about to boil over."

He whirled and grabbed the pan before the dark liquid could spill over. They looked at each other and busted out laughing. Tugging her back into his arms, he whispered, "See what you do to me."

"Make you ruin a good thing?"

"I sure hope not," he said, his thoughts already wandering ahead on this new path.

"I think it's ready," she replied, pointing to the rich drink.

Jon poured the steaming brew into two mugs and watched as she dropped marshmallows on top. "Perfect," she said.

He handed her a mug. "You haven't tasted it yet."

"I don't need to." Then she reached up and gave him a chaste kiss on the cheek. "No matter what, I'll never forget our *two* first dates."

Jon took that admission as a win. "Me either."

They sat and drank their cocoa while listening to a modern mix of country and classic rock music on the radio while they got to know each other more. When Lynsey looked up and noticed the rain had stopped, she jumped to her feet. "It's late and I need to go."

"I'll drive you back to the hotel."

"I can walk," she said, but she didn't look convincing.

"No, it's late and I am a gentleman."

Soon he had her in his little two-seater and back safely at the hotel. "I'll see you Saturday."

She leaned over and kissed him on the cheek. "Saturday, we dig for treasure."

Jon watched her go inside and wondered if he hadn't already found his treasure. As she'd said earlier, that was yet to be determined.

Chapter Seven

Saturday morning dawned clear but with a definite nip in the air. Lynsey dressed in old jeans and a University of Georgia sweatshirt then tossed a wool scarf around her neck. She always brought a large suitcase of clothes with her on these business excursions, since she usually drove to the places on the restoration roster. Everything from business attire to the work clothes she wore today so she could explore at will and get acclimated. All that work and exploration in far-flung towns was why she'd given up on dating. Usually if she got interested in a new person, she'd wind up having to leave for weeks at a time. And that would be that. Men couldn't understand or accept her work.

Another reason she shouldn't have kissed Jon the other night. She'd have to leave soon and then what? He'd go back to his self-imposed isolation and she'd dig into a new project down the road. Did she really want that for the rest of her life?

Maybe not, but these days she did want that promotion Richard kept dangling at her like the proverbial carrot. It would mean better pay and hours and more overseeing instead of doing the footwork. Today, she would bring up decorating Magnolia Manor, maybe even having an open house. Or better yet, what if they held a party at the manor?

She gasped at the idea that popped into her head as she headed downstairs to find caffeine and a couple of Danishes to take for breakfast with Jon.

A ball maybe? With a historical theme?

Would Jon go for that? Did they have time to plan that?

Her head filled with visions of sugarplums, Lynsey sipped her latte and strolled along toward the manor, giggling at that theme. It was like a manor house without all the servants. With only a lonely, gorgeous, studious, confused occupant who still suffered from losing a loving mother too soon and getting to know a distant father too late. Her heart always went to mush when she thought about Jon living there all alone. No wonder women swarmed around the man like honeybees. Who could resist that kind of challenge?

Apparently, she couldn't. Last night had proved that, but it was too late to take back the kisses. No work talk had led to small talk and then to more serious talk. They'd shared the kinds of things two people who trusted each other eventually shared. She only hoped she hadn't overshared about her middle-class childhood, her cheerleader days and her struggles during college. Her life hadn't been isolated or complicated or entitled.

Jon's life had been all of those things.

Maybe this purging today would help him.

Or she might ruin what could become a beautiful friendship.

When she reached the estate, Lynsey stood on the footpath near the lake and peered up at the mansion. She pictured the gazebo by the lake, now shining white thanks to several volunteers, decorated with greenery. Maybe some magnolia leaves and other natural elements, with white sparkling lights and big red bows and ribbons. Then she pictured the house with candles in every window—the modern kind that wouldn't burn down the house—and wreaths of greenery with more red bows on the many windows. Two parlor ferns by the double doors, decorated in twinkling lights. One of the cedar trees near the street all lit up with colorful lights. A big white gingerbread of a house that would shout, "'Tis the season to be jolly!"

Then she imagined the curtains pulled back and couples inside the large parlor, dancing in their finery. Could that actually happen? Would Jon hold her in his arms and kiss her again?

When the front door opened, Lynsey came out of her daydream and spotted him on the side porch with a puzzled expression on his face. She waved and followed the rock steps up to the house.

"Hi," he said, a cup of coffee in his hand. "What were you doing, standing in the cold?"

"Just thinking." She wasn't ready yet to shout out her elaborate plans. "The gazebo looks so much better and everyone is talking about Lettie and her Jonathon."

Giving her a quizzical frown, he asked, "Should I be scared about your thoughts?"

"Maybe. You never know what will pop into my head at any given moment."

Then she rattled the white bag in her hand to distract him. "I brought breakfast."

"Oh, good. I was about to butter toast."

"No need. I have a cream-cheese Danish and two apple fritters from the hotel bakery."

"You are too good to be true."

"And don't you forget it."

He guided her into the house. After handing her a cup of coffee, he started digging into the bag of pastries. "So we're really doing this?"

Lynsey grabbed two napkins. "Yes, unless you've reconsidered?"

"No. Ethel told me if we didn't do it, she'll force me next week." He chose an apple fritter and took a bite.

"Ethel means business."

"Yes." He didn't look enthused even if he had on an old blue T-shirt and worn jeans and looked ready to work. He placed the half-eaten fritter back on the napkin. "She's been after me for years to clean out the turret. My fairy godmother is a neat freak."

Lynsey touched his arm. "If you're uncomfortable—"

His gaze fell on Lynsey with a tormented hope. "No, I've put this off long enough."

"Cleaning and purging? Or facing the memories?"

"You really do understand me," he said. Putting down his coffee, he gave her his full attention. "I want you to know I appreciate your offer to help me. You have your reasons and I get that, but most of the women I've been involved with don't seem to like this place."

Lynsey chewed on her cream-cheese treat then shook her head. "That's hard to believe."

"One told me I should raze it and build a more modern house. The one she described sounded like one of those McMansions. You know the kind?"

"Yes, I do. And those are the modern-day version of this house."

"I never thought of it that way. Still."

"Still, I agree with you and it's not only because of why I'm in town. I have a very personal reason why I chose this line of work."

"Tell me," he said, grabbing a bite of fritter again. "We never got around to that last night."

"Because you said work was off-topic." And maybe because she hadn't been ready to talk about something so private and dear to her.

"Well, we're about to work, so tell me the whole story."

She took a deep breath. "My grandparents had a beautiful old house near where I grew up in Atlanta." Glancing out at the ducks and geese on the lake, she went on. "Their farmhouse wasn't anywhere near as grand as your home, but it was big and rambling and had a wraparound porch and all sorts of great hiding places. I loved going to stay with them during the summer. It was torn down when I was in high school."

Sympathy changed Jon's frown into a soft understanding. "Ah, so you're out to save these fading beauties?"

"Something like that, yes."

"I'm guessing you fought to save your grandparents' house?"

"I did but no one could save it. Granny and Papa had to move to an assisted living home and my parents didn't have the money to renovate the farmhouse. My grandparents needed any money they could get for medical bills and their living expenses."

She explained she tried by starting a petition which only made the grandfatherly mayor and the members of the city council laugh and pat her on the shoulder. It was too late. Unable to pay for the extra cost of retirement living that went beyond Social Security and Medicare, her grandparents had agreed to sell the house and acreage to a builder.

"He tore the house down and put up a shopping center."

Jon touched a hand to her shoulder. "Seems you have some memories to face, too."

She gave him a sincere, firm glance. "I did face them. Head-on."

Jon put his hands on her arms. "You did. You're still fighting to save that house, I think."

He was right about that. "Now I'm fighting to save this home and your town. I know things could easily go on as is, and everyone would survive somehow. You'll protect this home as long as you can, but one day you might decide you've had enough, and you need to decide how to handle that. Research indicates the houses along the lake do sell at times and most of the buyers seem content to respect the historical significance of these wonderful old homes. I've seen a lot of small towns just waste away while the citizens threw up their hands in defeat."

She glimpsed out toward the lake. "If everyone gives up, these homes will go one by one. I'd hate to see that happen."

"I'm not one of those citizens," he said, smiling at her. "You've shown me the light and I'm willing to do my best to help you come up with a plan that suits everyone in Springlake. Or at least those who haven't thrown up their hands and given up." Then he lifted a finger toward the gazebo in clear view. "In fact, the hard work is over. It's been fortified with solid, strong wood and is no longer a safety hazard. You and the Garden Club women should be able to decorate it soon."

Lynsey squealed in delight and hugged him tight. "Thank you, Jon. You won't regret this."

She pulled back and their eyes met. "Is it too early to kiss you?" he asked, his tone deep and husky.

Lynsey gave him his answer with a quick peck on the lips. "Never too early for that but we have work to do."

"Oh, I see. We're back to work?"

"You're not getting out of this."

He smiled and took her hand. "You brought your tote bag so I know this is serious."

"I want to take notes, get some pictures and search for hidden treasures. Especially Lettie's camera." She shrugged. "I'm expecting a lot of history and maybe some interesting artifacts. The more I know about the past of Springlake, the better I can create a workable plan for the future."

Jon gazed at her with an awestruck expression on his face. "You should use that statement at the next meeting, which will be the one where we vote."

"I will." Pointing up, she said, "I'll have more ammunition by then."

"Then let's get to it." He guided her up the hallway and after they'd trudged up two flights of stairs, he said, "I hope I don't have to move any heavy furniture today."

"We'll never know until we open the door," she replied,

pointing to the turret room a few feet away.

Jon gazed at her and then stared down the door. With a quick breath, he said, "Here goes nothing."

"Or here comes everything," Lynsey replied. Then she took his hand. "You're not alone, Jon. Okay?"

He nodded and squeezed her hand. "I understand that now more than ever."

Lynsey's enthusiasm had Jon stumped. She came alive when she talked about the past, her eyes animated with ideas and her hands lifting in the air. He couldn't remember the last time he'd seen anyone so fired up.

She'd taken his breath away and wrapped his heart in a warmth that left him confused. That, and considering she was the only person who could get him to explore the turret room, left him both elated and fearful.

He didn't know if he was ready to let go of his comfortable, complacent life and dive into the deep waters of the past with her.

"Jon?"

He shook his head and lifted the key to the turret out of his jeans pocket. "Just thinking, like you were earlier."

Lynsey dropped her worn leather tote on a nearby bench and dug out her cell and a notepad. "What are you thinking?"

"That I've been entombed in this old place for too long. That you are like some long-lost princess come to wake me up."

"Do you read fairy tales or romance novels?" she asked with a smile.

"No. Just law books and crime novels."

"Well, it would be a crime not to open this door for me." Then she gave him one of her beautiful smiles. "Comparing me to a princess is sweet and old-fashioned. I like that about you."

"You like that I'm old-fashioned? I'm also doddering, remember?"

She shook her head and laughed. "Just unlock the door already."

Jon took out the key and did as she asked, then took a deep breath. "Pandora's box is open, Princess Lynsey."

Lynsey stood while he pushed at the heavy creaking door, her eyes widening with each inch. Jon couldn't stop his smile. Teasing her with a slow reveal, he laughed when she gave him a frown. Then he opened the door and watched as her hands went to her mouth.

"Oh, my."

"What is it?" He turned to stare into the room, thinking she'd found a skeleton or at least a rat. Then he saw it. A dress hanging on some sort of mannequin.

"That is beautiful," she said as she rushed into the musty smelling room to see the dress up close. The scent of lavender mingled with a hint of moth balls. "And the Judy is ancient—I'd say late eighteen-hundreds."

"Excuse me," he replied. "The Judy?"

"The dress form," she said. "Seamstresses and designers use them to model and measure clothing and to make patterns, but the ones today are not this detailed."

Jon marched to the dress form. "Well, hello, Judy. So glad to meet you. What have you been doing with yourself lately? Just hanging out?"

Lynsey held her phone up and snapped a picture. "Oh, this will be perfect."

Jon whirled around. "Perfect for what?"

"Social media."

"You're going to put a picture of me talking to a dress form on social media."

"Yes, for publicity."

"Why do we need publicity?"

She didn't answer right away. Instead she hurried to touch the ruby-red dress with a sheer lacy black overlay on the hem, bodice, and sleeves. "This is exquisite. It looks like a ball gown. What if it belonged to Lettie?"

Jon enjoyed watching her as she studied the intricate design of the dress. "It might have. I remember when my mom found it in a box in the attic with dried lavender protecting it. I wonder how it wound up in here."

"Someone must have shoved it aside a long ago. But you said this was your father's office once?"

Jon nodded and moved further into the room, but found it hard to breathe. That slight scent of lavender brought back memories. "Let me crack a window and get rid of some of this stale air."

After he'd struggled with one of the tall, narrow windows, he turned to face Lynsey. "In his later years, Dad wasn't able to maneuver the stairs. We moved him to a downstairs bedroom with a view of the lake. He had a hospital bed and nurses around the clock while I was still working in Tallahassee."

He went quiet, the memories gathering around him like cobwebs. Then he looked out the window he'd forced open. "He had dementia. He didn't tell anyone at first, not even Ethel. She figured it out and called me home since he was becoming difficult to handle. I came back and stayed with him in the last months of his life."

Stayed with him and tried to straighten out the mess his father's finances had become due to people taking advantage and his dad's inability to pull together two thoughts in the last years of his life.

"I wish I'd known sooner but he was stubborn till the end."

Lynsey let go of the elbow-length sleeve of the dress and pivoted, her expression full of compassion, her eyes misty. "I'm so sorry, Jon. That must have been so horrible."

He nodded, swallowed the pain and anger. "He had too

much pride but in those last days, he had lucid moments where he'd laugh with me and tell me stories. I slept downstairs to be near him. Of course, we had all kinds of alarms and locks on the doors. He once tried to go out on the lake in a skiff during a rainstorm because he thought my mother was waiting for him down by the gazebo. I couldn't abandon him."

"No, you did the right thing," she said. "So you gave up a lucrative practice in a big law firm to come back home?"

"I did." He took in the fresh air, breathing deeply as the weight seemed to lift off his shoulders. "You're the only person who's ever acknowledged that. Everyone else just assumed I wanted to come back. I thought I'd return to the firm and make partner. After a bad breakup, I settled in, guarding this old place like a lonely sentinel."

Lynsey tugged at her shirt. "Been there, done that. And I've disrupted your tranquility."

"No," he said, "you've made me see how lonely and isolated I'd become. I see the same people every day and share small talk, work with everyone in town when needed, even doing pro bono at times. I've tried to be a part of keeping this community alive, but I haven't done much other than show up and make lame suggestions." Going to the roll-top desk centered on one side of the room he gave Lynsey a broad smile. "Until you showed up and brought me out of my stupor."

"So you don't resent me or think I'm a pest?"

"No, I don't resent you. I'm thankful for you, pest that you are."

She studied him, her eyes moving over his face. "Maybe you needed an outsider to talk to, someone who doesn't have a vested interest in the history of your family."

"Maybe so," he said. "Or maybe Jonathon and Lettie wanted me to find the kind of happiness they found all those years ago."

"Do you think you'll be happy once I rearrange

Springlake and change it?"

"I'm glad for that, but mostly I'll be happy that I met someone who sees me so clearly." He studied the dress then looked at Lynsey. "Someone who'll have to leave eventually, however."

Lynsey stood on the other side of the circular room while he stood behind the desk. For a moment, they didn't speak. Time seemed to stand still. Jon could almost hear the music of the past, could picture her in this dress, dancing with him.

"We don't have to finish this today," she said. "The dress is a treasure and I'd like to explore its history but I won't involve you." Touching a hand to the black lace collar, she said, "We'll display it ... somewhere."

"I don't want to finish this," he admitted. "I want to start it. Right here, right now."

Then he came around the desk. "Let's find some more treasures."

Chapter Eight

Lynsey didn't try to hide her surprise. After his comment, she wasn't confident about what she should say or do. "Okay. Are you sure?"

"Yes," he said, hurrying toward the desk. "I'll start on the desk and you can take some of the files inside the credenza."

Lynsey watched him, noticing the frantic way he seemed to be going about this. She went to the tall, elegant Italian-style credenza and opened one of the creaky doors. Books and papers slid out onto the worn carpet. Lynsey plopped down on the floor and started sorting and searching. Laws books and financial records, old letters and a set of some sort of books lay piled at her feet.

"This place is a mess," Jon said after he settled into the stiff wooden chair. "No wonder my father was so moody. This chair isn't all that comfortable."

"Neither is this floor," she replied, wondering if going through the motions when he didn't want to be here was wise. Maybe he did need to get this out of his system. She wished she could get *him* out of her system. Sounded like he was still pining for someone else.

For a while, they worked in silence. Lynsey tried to find a way to tell him about her elaborate plans for the Christmas Ball, but now wasn't the time. Would there be a good time?

Or was he right? She'd seal this deal and move on. No parties, no celebrations beyond applause at the last meeting?

After clearing out what needed to be thrown away, Jon went down to get a huge trash bag. They filled it quickly with old receipts and mail, placing anything that looked interesting or noteworthy on the desktop he'd cleaned off.

Lynsey stacked law books and crime novels on the floor by the credenza, then reached for the other books that had fallen out.

"Jon," she said, after opening a couple of the leather-bound books, "these aren't textbooks books or novels. They're journals of some sort."

Jon stood and came over to sit on the floor next to her. "Journals? Whose?"

Lynsey studied the faded initials etched in gold. "A. T."

Jon took one of the half-dozen journals and opened it to stare at some of the writing. Then he glanced toward the dress form they'd moved to one side. "Abigail Townsend."

"Who is that?" Lynsey asked, excited.

He got up and lifted the other journals off the floor. "My mother," he said, taking the worn books, each tied with a strip of leather, to the desk. "Private."

Lynsey's heart sank. She couldn't force him to let her read his mother's intimate thoughts. "I understand." When he didn't speak, she said, "I'm going to finish up for now. We made some progress and I've found some interesting maps and tidbits to use at our next meeting. Christmas is a few weeks away and I have so much to do."

He didn't seem to be listening. He sat staring at the journals.

Lynsey gathered her things and turned to face him. "Jon, I'm going."

"Okay. Go do what you need to get finished. See you later."

They hadn't found Lettie's old camera, but she didn't think that mattered right now. She gave him one last look and made her way downstairs, leaving by the back door so she could take the lake path to the hotel. The sunshine should have warmed her but Lynsey couldn't stop the fear clawing at her heart. Why did she have to always push people to do her biding? She shouldn't have forced him to go up into the turret room.

And she'd been unable to answer him after he'd said she'd leave eventually.

She would need to leave soon. She'd be back to oversee and check on the renovations. If this town would agree to revitalize. If this man wanted to see her again.

Had Jon known the journals were stored in this room? If so, he could have moved them so she'd never find them. No, he'd been shocked, his face turning pale, his expression becoming guarded and tight. Would he sit and read his mother's words, hoping for something, seeking something he needed to know?

Not sure what to do, she left the path and walked up the hill toward the main street, crossing the railroad tracks that ran through the heart of the town. It didn't take long to reach the Springlake Hotel. The big red-brick building took up a whole block.

She decided to go straight up to her room and order room service. She needed some peace and quiet.

After talking to community leaders and meeting with various committees and sub-committees along with property owners all week, she'd given her best pitches. If they couldn't put together this Christmas Ball and hold it at the mansion to draw more supporters, her hard work might not pay off. How could she do that with Jon in a mood and time running out? The ball would need to be before the next meeting. Everyone present would cast a vote, and that was coming up the week before Christmas.

She entered the elegant lobby of the old hotel. Deep blue-velvet high-backed chairs and settees, with parlor palms arranged on each side, graced the central location in front of the massive fireplace. Lynsey headed toward the wide mahogany staircase then heard someone calling her name.

Ethel Porter waved from the café entrance and then came out to greet her. "Lynsey, how did it go in the turret room?"

Lynsey checked around for prying eyes and big ears. "Not so well."

Ethel took one look at her face and said, "I was about to grab a bite to eat. Come and join me and we'll talk."

Lynsey almost said no, but she needed to understand why Jon seemed so shocked and why he'd recoiled from her after she'd found his mother's journal. Who would know better than this woman?

"I'm not hungry," she said. "I do need someone to talk to though, about a lot of things."

Ethel pursed her lips and then said, "We'll find a quiet corner and after I order a chicken salad sandwich, I'll tell the waiter to leave us alone."

Lynsey was too shaken to say no. Thankfully, the lunch crowd had dissipated, and they had no one around them once they were settled at a corner table with a nice view of the lake in the distance.

Ethel, prim and proper, ordered two chicken salad sandwiches and two hot Earl Grey teas. Lynsey didn't argue with her. Instead, she sat staring at the portraits lining the walls where burgundy vinyl café booths made a symmetric display.

"What did he do?" Ethel asked, her tone motherly and comforting.

Lynsey let out a sigh. "Well, when I finally got him up there, the first thing we found was a beautiful old formal gown."

"Oh, the dress," Ethel said as she placed a white linen napkin on her lap, "I had one of the handymen move it after Mr. Townsend saw it and had a meltdown. It was once displayed in Abigail's small office downstairs but it kept scaring the cleaning service people. After he got so emotional over it, I decided to hide it as far away as possible." Looking down at her plate, she added, "I never thought about how Jon might react to seeing it again."

Lynsey realized the dress had played a part in the Townsend family's tragedy. "So you know of the dress?"

"It's rumored Lettie wore it to a Christmas Ball when she was falling in love with her Jonathon. But I've never seen any proof of that."

"How did it survive this long?" Lynsey asked. "It's in good shape, all things considered."

"Abigail—Jon's mother—found it in the attic and took it to a dry-cleaning service in Pensacola that treated and preserved ball gowns and wedding dresses. She had it cleaned and tidied up and mended with her specific instructions. For a while, it was sealed in a protective box. Before she died, Abigail found that old dress form and put the dress on it. She loved showing it off and she always kept a lavender plant growing by the window. After her death, it only brought back memories for Jon's daddy." Ethel stopped for a moment and took a breath. "He never liked the smell of lavender after she passed."

"The dress does smell of lavender," Lynsey replied, her mind centered on the ball gown. "Maybe that's what put Jon in a mood, too."

The waiter brought their hot tea and the dainty crustless sandwiches along with a bowl of fruit and two vanilla petit fours.

After she'd mixed cream into her tea, Ethel glanced over at Lynsey. "Did Jon get upset after seeing the dress?"

"No," Lynsey said, taking a sip of the tea. "He seemed to enjoy finding it. I think the whole purging thing got to him and then ... I found some journals."

Ethel put down her sandwich and held a hand to her mouth. "Abigail's journals."

"Yes." Lynsey nibbled on a grape. "That's when he got quiet and moved himself and the journals to the desk. I'm not even sure he noticed when I left."

Ethel stirred her tea again. "They never got over her sudden death. A heart attack and in the prime of her life. She married her Jonathon at twenty-five, had Jon at thirty and died at forty-five."

"That would be hard to accept," Lynsey replied. "He did open up and tell me a few things but ... I'm not sure I should push him on anything else right now."

Ethel's soft smile hid a lot and told Lynsey nothing. "You mean, regarding the revitalization or how he feels about you?"

"I'm not sure what you're saying."

"Honey, anyone can see you two caused sparks to fly the first minute he laid eyes on you. He changed almost immediately and actually started paying attention to what this town is trying to do."

"He has been helpful, showing me the house, inviting me to dinner and, yes, we've grown close, but he's holding back." He told me he doesn't like change and ... I'm a big change. I can see how that would affect him."

Ethel touched her hand. "You can't give up, Lynsey. Most of us want this and we're pulling for the committee we put in charge to make the right decision. Tell me what you have planned. I heard the Garden Club is excited about decorating the gazebo now that it's been renovated. I missed the meeting the other morning but Jon made good on getting the work done."

Before she knew it, Lynsey had poured out her plans in vivid details. "The gazebo renovation is great, yet I still have to get the plans for the ball firmed up. The committee meets again on the Tuesday before Christmas and I'm running out of time. I want to hold this event as soon as possible so we can display the entire plan I've been working on with my team back in Atlanta. I have until the first of the year to get this done."

Ethel ate her food with a peace and calm that amazed

Lynsey. She, on the other hand, had picked at the delicate little sandwich and tried some of the fruit. The petit four screamed at her so she gulped it down in one bite and then regretted that.

"I like your ideas," Ethel said. "But you're right. It takes time to plan such an event, but we can pull it off with a little ingenuity. We'll keep the food simple—appetizers and punch. I know a caterer who can whip that up once we get a head count. The church orchestra ensemble will be glad to play at the event, once we pick a date. That just leaves invitations. I do have some influence. I can hint to Jon, too. He listens to me."

"I thought I'd talk to him about this today but that didn't happen," Lynsey replied. "I can't push him. He's already having a hard time dealing with all of this."

"He's dealing with the grief he's held for so long, honey. This isn't your fault. I know he cares about you but this change is bringing up things he's kept hidden away. You've made him smile a lot lately though. He still chuckles about that run-in you had with Lucy."

"I have more to worry about than that goose," Lynsey said. "My goose will be cooked if I don't make this happen."

"Well, we can't have that. You talk to Jon again when he's in a better mood and let me handle the rest." Ethel sipped the rest of her tea. "I do have one question. After you succeed, what will you do?"

Lynsey blinked and gave her friend a long stare. "I'll move on."

"Exactly," Ethel said. "Think about what that might do to Jon. Knowing that could be the reason he's suddenly holding back." The older woman leaned close. "He was involved with a woman in Tallahassee. She wanted nothing more than to show him off and use his name and money to move her up the social scales. You are nothing like her."

After they parted ways, with Ethel assuring her things would work out, Lynsey started toward her room again, her mind on Ethel's warning and what Jon had said while they were in the turret room. What would happen after she'd accomplished her mission?

When she saw Wendell Norton coming out of the bar, she hesitated. The man set off all sort of alarms each time she was around him.

"Lynsey," he said, tugging her into a hug, "where you headed?"

"Upstairs," she said, extracting herself out of his too-familiar embrace and the smell of alcohol on his breath. "I have a lot of work to do."

"What? It's the weekend. Why don't you let me give you a tour of the town? Or better yet, we could head to Pensacola for some real fun."

"I can't, Wendell," she said, backing against a chair. "I really need to work."

His smile turned into a sneer. "Oh, so you can have dinner with Jon and help him clean out the cobwebs in the attic," he said with a wink. "But you can't be seen with me?"

"What I do is none of your business," she said, backing away so she could scoot by him. "I have to go."

Wendell didn't take the hint. Pulling her close, he said, "Hey, c'mon. Forget I said that and let's admit we need to get together."

"No," she said, louder this time. "Let me go."

Wendell sneered at her again.

A shove sent Wendell against the wall. Jon held him by the shoulders, pinning him. "You heard Lynsey. She said no."

"Hi, Jon," Wendell said. "I sure didn't hear her say no. I heard a maybe."

Jon leaned in, pressing his hands against Wendell's jacket. "I heard her tell you to let her go. You need to respect that request and leave."

Looking surprised and angry, Wendell tried to twist away. "So you're her hero now, Jon? Her protector? Where have you been this whole time while we've been working to save this town?"

"I've been right here," Jon replied on a deadly calm note. "And I'm not going anywhere. But you are. I'll see to that."

By then the hotel security had been alerted and Wendell was escorted out the back door toward the only cab in town.

Jon turned back to Lynsey. She stood in a corner, mortified and knowing this wouldn't go over very well.

"Are you okay?" he asked, his tone low, his eyes full of anger and alarm.

Lynsey straightened and nodded. "I'm fine. I was handling the situation."

"So I could tell."

"Thank you for defending me, Jon. Now the whole town will hear about this."

Jon ran a hand over his hair. "I don't care about that and I told you, you shouldn't either."

"My job is on the line." Lynsey shook her head. "I really need to go upstairs."

"Lynsey, wait," he said, his gaze holding hers. "I came to apologize. Can we talk?"

"Do you want to talk? I mean really talk?"

"Yes. I was rude earlier. Seeing those journals shook me."

Remembering her talk with Ethel, she finally nodded. "We have a lot to discuss but not here and not at your house." Then she lowered her head. "First, I need a couple of hours to myself."

Dejected, he asked, "Want to go for a drive later then?"

She nodded. "I'll meet you out front."

He checked his watch. "I'll be back to pick you up at four."

Lynsey hurried upstairs, her head down. That scene just now wouldn't bode well for the next committee meeting. Thinking she'd made a mess of everything, she shut the door to her room and fell across the bed. Richard had sent her to do the job she'd always done so well. Why had this project turned into a big fail?

Maybe because she'd allowed her heart to turn into a pile of mush for a man who didn't want her to mess with the grief he held so close?

Two hours later, Jon pulled his car up to the front of the Springlake Hotel. After explaining to the valet that he was waiting for someone, he kept glancing at the steps leading down to the sidewalk. The hotel thrived because of booking large events such as weddings, rehearsal dinners and anniversary parties. It certainly fit the Victorian and Queen Anne eras with its own big rounded turret that was now used as a bridal suite.

He thought of Lynsey. He shouldn't be picturing her in a white dress as she came down the grand staircase of the hotel. She would be leaving soon, and he'd been too infatuated to realize that. No more kisses or pretending they had something special. Being in his father's old office today and seeing the red dress and finding his mother's journals had left him exhausted with pent-up grief.

Now, he wanted to tell Lynsey all that was on his heart and explain to her that he couldn't do this. He couldn't watch someone else walk out of his life.

But when she came out the door, her hair lifting in the brisk wind, her eyes downcast and her expression firm and unyielding, he knew he wouldn't have to tell her anything.

She already knew.

Chapter Nine

"I wanted so much," Lynsey said while they drove south toward the coast. "I wanted to wear that dress and throw a big party at your house and show the whole town what I can do to make it the best small town in Florida." Sniffing back the tears she refused to cry, she shook her head. "Then today, I realized it's already the best little town in Florida. It's full of vibrant, caring people like Ethel and my new friend Amy and even the women in the Garden Club. I really didn't want to change it, Jon. I wanted to make it better."

He'd let her talk, let her go on and on. She talked about the mayor and how even if Kathryn Barton had her own agenda, she really did want Springlake to thrive. She told him about going to the post office and taking Paul Caldwell's lighthearted barbs and sitting with Stella Scott while Stella gave her a rundown of the complete history of the town.

"They all had one thing in common. They care about your family and this town. That's all anyone can ask, right?"

He nodded but he didn't respond.

So she said what she knew he needed to say. "We both know this had to end. I shouldn't have pushed you on the gazebo or anything else. I shouldn't have let things get this far—the dinners, the kisses, that amazing hot cocoa you make—"

"Lynsey, stop," Jon finally said. "Just please stop. You've changed my life, changed my attitude, and I'm pretty sure this small-town revitalization plan is going to go through. Everyone I've talked to agrees you're the real deal."

Shocked, Lynsey wondered why that praise and promise didn't make her want to scream with glee. Instead she stared out the window as they took Scenic Highway 90 around the bay, the water below the bluffs blue and choppy.

"I might be good at bringing small towns into this century, but I'm not so great in the relationship department. Once I know the vote is solid and Springlake is ready to be recreated, I'm going back to Atlanta, Jon. Before I hurt you even more."

Jon didn't respond. The minutes ticked by like hours while the silence in the small car stretched between them until finally he stopped the car at a bayside park and turned off the engine.

"I have so many things I need to say," he admitted. "I can't find the words." Then he turned to her and touched his fingers to her hair, his eyes full of everything he held in his heart. "I'm sorry, Lynsey. About everything. I thought I was ready but…I'm not."

"Then take me back to the hotel," Lynsey replied. "Take me back and I'll finish what I started. That's what I'm good at, after all."

The next week came too quickly. Lynsey filed paperwork and sent e-mails back and forth to her team in Atlanta, reporting to Richard though calls and messages that she was ninety-five percent sure they'd get the nod to revitalize Springlake.

She walked down to the water Monday afternoon and

saw that the Garden Club had taken over the gazebo, adding poinsettias, garlands, and wreaths. The fresh sparkling white structure shouted Christmas. Tears came to her eyes when she went inside to touch her fingers to the heart with the initials JT and LM centered there, still intact with a wooden frame built to protect it. She hadn't talked to Jon since he'd dropped her back off at the hotel, both of them sad and confused. She'd heard he might be going out of town for the holidays, as he usually did.

Opening up that little room had released a storm of emotions for both of them.

Too many to contain now that they both realized things were ending.

On Tuesday afternoon, she put on her best wool suit and black pumps and made her way downstairs to catch a ride with Ethel to the Assembly House. The vote would take place there today. Wendell Norton had filed a report against Jon, claiming he'd been assaulted. Several witnesses had disputed that so Wendell had been fired by the mayor and the town was now looking for a new city planner. Virginia Montgomery had replaced him on the Planning Committee.

Ethel greeted her with a wide smile. "You look lovely, Lynsey."

"Thank you." Lynsey didn't dare ask if Jon would be at the meeting. She didn't expect him.

Ethel drove her economy car the short distance to the white, sprawling building that to this day still held Assembly Conferences that included writers and artists, philosophers and politicians. Today, this little town might be changed forever.

Once they were inside, the wide windows allowing a stunning view of the lake, Lynsey noticed the large space was standing-room only. Had everyone in town come out for this vote?

Not everyone. She didn't see Jon.

The meeting was called to order and the mayor stood

and explained what was about to happen. "We've seen the plans. We've heard Lynsey Milton's ideas. We've discussed the pros and cons of revitalizing our beautiful Springlake. We've solicited and secured private, city, and state funding and we've received several grants. It's time to take a vote. You each have an official ballot. You either vote for or against and come one by one and drop your choice inside this locked box on the podium table. We have a committee standing by to tally the votes and we'll know before we leave today whether this passes or not."

Lynsey stood and plied her case once again. After she'd shown the updated plans for downtown Springlake, she thanked everyone and sat back down to wait.

And wonder where Jon had gone.

Soon all the votes had been cast and the committee had moved to a corner to count the votes, with a supervisor watching every count. Lynsey didn't think she could stay in this room. She needed some fresh air. But too late. The counting committee was almost finished.

The mayor called out. "Any more votes before we tally?"

"One more," came a voice from the back of the room.

Lynsey knew that voice. She glanced at Ethel and then turned to see.

Jon walked calmly up front and leaned over to write his choice. Then he walked to the committee members waiting in the corner. "The last one."

Lynsey watched as he then turned and left the room without another word.

Ethel's frown said it all. He'd vote for change. That didn't mean he was ready to change his personal life.

The next morning Lynsey packed up and ready to leave.

It was over and she'd won. The residents of Springlake, Florida had passed the vote to renovate their small town, and by a high margin at that.

But her joy hadn't gone off the meters and her heart wasn't really all that excited. She'd won the town over yet she'd lost the man who'd made her feel alive.

The man she'd fallen in love with. She didn't even know how to ask God for help. Did she deserve to be in love and happy?

After checking out, Lynsey got into her car and started toward Highway 90. Then she decided to take one more drive around the lake. She needed to see the gazebo one last time.

With dawn cresting to the east, Lynsey got out of the car and walked down to the gazebo, glad it was early, and no one was on the path.

When she again saw the stark white structure shimmering with tiny white lights and decorated with green garland, she gasped and put a hand to her mouth. Tears pierced her eyes worse than the morning cold as she smiled at the poinsettias and the magnolia leaves mixed in with the garland.

She went inside the gazebo and saw Lucy and her entourage circling the water.

"So beautiful."

"Yes, it is."

Lynsey whirled to find Jon there holding a big white box. Her heart hammered a sharp beat and she had to take in a breath. "I didn't mean to disturb you."

"I was waiting for you," he said. "Ethel told me you were leaving early this morning."

"And you knew I'd come by here?"

"I hoped," he admitted. "I didn't want to ship this to Atlanta."

He handed her the box. "Don't open this yet. I know you have to go, but Lynsey, can you come back for Christmas?"

Perplexed, she asked, "Why?"

"Just promise me you'll come back on Christmas Eve, please?"

"Because you'll be gone?"

"No, because I'll be home. Waiting."

Then he turned and went back up to his castle on the hill.

Lynsey got in the car and left, but in her heart she knew she'd be back.

A week later, she once again stood out on the lake path, wearing the ruby-red ball gown that Jon had given her, a black wool cape covering her from the icy weather. The dress had been in the box along with Lettie's camera which was safe in her hotel room for now. She stood and stared in amazement at the house before her.

Magnolia Manor was all dressed up for Christmas, with a wreath and a candle in every window and a big, sparkling Christmas tree lighting up the sunroom and another one on the open porch next to it. She had the hotel taxi bring her to the front of the house but when she'd seen the decorations, she'd hurried around to the lake side.

The house was full of people, laughing and talking and moving through the rooms.

Her Christmas Ball.

Tears misted along with the rare light dusting of snow the weatherman had predicted. While she stood shivering and thanking God for Jon Townsend, she saw him walking down the back terrace toward her.

Without thinking, Lynsey hurried toward him and they met in the yard.

"You came back," he said, taking her into his arms. "I wasn't sure."

"I wasn't either," she admitted, until I opened the box. "I

realized some men communicate with words and some with actions. Your gift told me what I needed to know."

He laughed and touched her upswept hair then opened her cape to look at the sparkling black lace on the ruby-red dress. "That I love you and want you to stay?"

"Yes," she whispered. "Yes."

"Is that a yes, you know I love you or a yes, you love me, too, and you want to stay."

"All of the above," she said. "What made you do all of this?"

"You," he admitted. "And the journals my mother left to me but I never saw. She told the story of Lettie and Jonathon and this dress. And the story of her love for my father and me. She wanted me to have that kind of love. Then Ethel and I had a come-to-Jesus meeting where I saw the light."

"And now I can see all the lights of Christmas. It's beautiful, Jon."

"I had to pay double to hire people to get this done and move furniture around so we'd have room to dance, but it was so worth it."

Lynsey smiled at him and hugged him close. "I do love you. And I quit my job. I hear Springlake is looking for city planner."

"I know the perfect one." He kissed her hair. "But tonight, I want to hold you and dance with you while I thank God for His amazing restorations."

Lynsey agreed. "Let's go before Lucy comes at me again."

He nodded. "Later, we have a date inside the gazebo. After all, our initials are carved there for eternity."

"Forever," she said, touching a hand to his cheek. "Just like Jonathon and his Lettie."

Together, they walked toward the glittering mansion ... and toward the future in the best little town in Florida.

A member of the Romance Writers of America and American Christian Fiction Writers Honor Rolls, Lenora Worth writes romance and romantic suspense for Harlequin's Love Inspired and sweet romance for Tule Publishing. Her books have finaled in the ACFW Carol Awards. She also received the Romantic Times Pioneer Award for Inspirational Fiction. Lenora is a NY Times, USA Today and Publishers Weekly bestselling writer and a 2019 RWA RITA® Finalist. With eighty-plus books published and over three million books in print, she enjoys adventures with her retired husband and loves reading, baking and shopping … especially shoe shopping.

Connect with her at http://www.lenoraworth.com/, @lenoraworth Twitter, https://www.pinterest.com/lenoraworth/, https://www.facebook.com/lenoraworthbooks/

Made in the USA
Lexington, KY
11 December 2019

58421071R00114